D1743098

REAPER OF WATER

THE ARTIFACT REAPER SAGA

JEN L. GREY

Created with Vellum

1

I shut the door as I step out of the bathroom. A flush of air brushes around me. Since absorbing the Flame of Hell a week ago, everything has changed. My vision seems sharper, which is saying something. In general, reapers have some of the best vision of any supernaturals due to the nature of our work. But now, even the air has an aura to it I can see as it blows past me. And as if that's not strange enough, it feels somehow connected to me.

If someone had told me over a week ago how the third artifact would change me, I would have told them they were crazy... but not anymore.

Now, with three of the artifacts – the Earth Crystal, Angel's Breath, and Hell's Flame – coursing through me, it's fundamentally altered me. I hope it's for the better, but who the hell knows? One thing is for certain; I won't be bowing down to the council, demons, or anyone else any longer.

My power thrums inside of me as I stand in the middle of my studio. The dark couch Charlie and I retrieved from the dumpster is five feet away to the left, and the round kitchen table I bought at a yard sale is two feet to the right.

So, I have plenty enough room to have a little fun. This is my favorite part of having these powers.

I hold my hand out, palm facing upward, and I bring my fingers toward me and into a fist. The air responds and begins twirling in front of me, connecting deep inside me. It's as if I can feel it spinning in my core.

One of the things I've learned is that each element has its own color of magic. As the wind spins in front of me, the blue of the Angel's Breath inside me pulses, but the brown strand from the Earth Crystal flows in sync as well as the purple of the Flame of Hell. Yes, the purple threw me off at first, but since the Flame was both half red and half blue, I guess it makes sense that when combined, it would be a vibrant shade of purple. What's even more surprising is that for once, my reaper magic doesn't bother me. It's as if the warmth of the Flame balances out the coldness. I've never been so comfortable in my skin. I can see what a reaper's place is really meant to be; a passage so a soul can get to its final resting place. There isn't anything evil to it, and it took until now for me to realize that.

As I lower my hand, the small tornado lowers with it. The wind stays at the same height as my fist. I'm now able to control my powers in small increments. Anything too large I'm still not comfortable with.

A loud knock at the door startles me and my hands drop. The small tornado hits the ground and begins making its way to my feet. Gathering my bearings just in time, I open my hands wide, dissipating it back into the air.

The door opens, and Charlie peers into the room. "Everything okay in here?"

Why do I feel like he asks me that all of the time? "Yeah, I was just practicing." I shake my head and place my hands on my hips. "Why do you knock when you have a key?"

"Because you still need your privacy." He steps through the door, his hazel eyes sparkling. "And I'm a gentleman." He holds out a bouquet of sunflowers.

Wait... "Are those for me?" I've never had someone buy flowers for me before. A grin spreads across my face.

"This would be really awkward right now if they weren't." He runs a hand through his short blond hair and chuckles. "Do you not want them?"

Oh... shit. I must seem ungrateful. "Of course I do." I walk over to him and kiss his lips as I take the flowers from him. "It's just I've never gotten anything like this before. Thank you. I love them."

"Anything for you." He reaches out and runs his fingers through my hair. "I want to be your first for all things."

"Well, you've certainly been that." God, I don't know what I would do without him. I lean in and kiss him again, focusing my energy on him. It's strange because even kissing Charlie feels different now. His lips feel softer yet still firm, and his breath makes me lightheaded. I moan as I deepen the kiss and hold the flowers out as I press against him.

He and I are the only things that matter right now. I open my mouth to slide my tongue against his lips. He groans and tugs on the ends of my hair when something coarse and prickly rubs against my arm.

"What the hell?" I pull away and look down. Holy shit. The sunflower has grown twice the size, and the vines are now wrapping around my arm. "I didn't even know I was doing that."

He laughs and takes the bouquet from me. "I better go put these up before you make them even bigger. Then they won't even fit on the table any longer." He taps me on the nose with a finger from his free hand at he passes by me.

It's funny because he's trying to act so lighthearted and

fun, but doesn't he realize I know him? I can see how tense is he right now and how that was one of his fake laughs. That's the same kind of laugh he'd have with the teachers at school when they would talk to him and go on and on about how great of a reaper he was back then. "You seem tense."

"What?" He sets the plant on the table and takes a deep breath before turning around. When he faces me, he relaxes his shoulders and sits in the chair.

Yeah, he's not fooling me. "Did something happen before you got here?"

"Not at all." He licks his bottom lip and leans back in the chair. "Just have a lot on my mind."

The air around him turns a shade darker, almost as if a storm is rolling in, but the weather outside is sunny with not a cloud in sight. Whatever is going on inside him is affecting the elements around him. "Is there anything I can do to help?"

He stands and shakes his head. "Don't worry. You have enough going on without adding me to your ever-growing list." He brushes his lips over mine and pulls away. "Everything is fine, and I'm going to make you breakfast now." He taps me on the nose and turns his back to me as he heads into the kitchen.

I'm not sure how much to push, but it's obvious that something is worrying him. I have a feeling it's me. It's only a matter of time before my powers begin to go out of sync again. They're going to until all four artifacts are running through me. We both know that, so time is of the essence.

A dark blue hue surrounds him as he pulls out pans to cook French toast. The negative energy connects to me and courses through my body.

I haven't told him about this yet, and I'm not sure now is the right time. It's strange because it's as if I'm looking at him through the eyes of the artifacts themselves. I would never be able to see the magnitude of his apprehension otherwise. Prior to absorbing the artifacts, I would know something was off, but not to this extent.

As Charlie puts egg-soaked bread in the pan, sweet vanilla fills the air, its scent sharper than ever before. Without much concentration, I can identify each individual smell in the air. Vanilla, eggs, yeast, and cinnamon, among others.

It's captivating, but at the same time, I wonder... what am I becoming? Yes, I'm more powerful, and I see things in a different light, but at what cost? I'm not sure what's happening to me.

2

After taking the last bite of my French toast, I place my fork on the plate. My belly is so full I feel like I'm about to burst, but there is no way I'm not going to finish the last bite of bliss. The cinnamon and vanilla are one of my favorite combinations, and I love that Charlie always cook with that in mind.

"Well, I would ask if you're full, but you had more than me, so I think you're good." Charlie's grin is big, and his shoulders shake with laughter.

"No judging." I motion around the room, causing a slight breeze. "This is a judgment free zone just like those gyms you see on tv." The sunflowers rustle.

His eyes lose a little of the warmth they held, and he huffs, tapping the table with his fingers. "Did you mean to do that?"

"Do what?" Crap, I didn't even notice that I'm using them.

"The wind blows outside, not inside without the aid of a fan or something." He rubs his hands together and looks around my entire apartment. "I don't see anything like that in here, so that only leaves you to cause it. So, I want to make sure you're feeling all right."

That's the horrible thing about a studio apartment. You can see the whole living space from one spot. My apartment isn't big and not the nicest, but this is the first place I've had that's all mine. The only thing that distinguishes the kitchen from the other areas is the linoleum flooring. The rest is covered in dingy gray carpet. Then, there is my couch and TV, and at the far end, the bed that was left behind by the prior renter. It's small but plenty of room for just me.

"Yeah, I'm fine. It's part of me." I don't want to lie to him, and it's kind of true. It's all connected to me now. I need to change the subject and fast. "So what are you doing today?"

"I've got to head into work." He glances down at his phone and frowns. "And I should probably get going. How 'bout I bring home some Mexican food for dinner tonight?"

"Sounds perfect." I hate that he must go to work. But Luke wants me to head over to the mansion today, and it would be best to go alone. I need to talk to him about what's going on with me, and I would downplay it if Charlie was there.

He stands and takes the few steps toward me. "Just be careful, okay?" He bends down and presses his lips to mine. "I don't know what I would do if something happened to you."

"Nothing is going to happen." I reach out and squeeze his hand. "I'll be right here when you get back."

"I love you. Call me if you need me." He gives me one last glance before he leaves.

When the door shuts, I let out a breath I didn't even realize I was holding. The truth of the matter is that I'm worried about my connection with the elements around me. For once, I'd like to be in control.

My phone rings from the corner of my room, and I rush over to the coffee table and pick it up. When I glance down, I find a text from Dax.

Hey Hot Stuff - Luke wants you to come here and check in.

I can't help the snort that escapes me. He's been giving me a hard time ever since I killed all of the demons down in hell with flames that came out my hands. But this text is timely. Luke may be able to give me some answers I'm needing anyway.

I picture Luke's office at the mansion and remove the barriers between my apartment and his place just like he taught me. The air begins to swirl around me, and soon the walls are so thick I can't see through them. The floor disappears, and I begin to drop, but now I'm able to control my speed. At least there are some small blessings.

Soon, something firm forms underneath me, and the wall of thick air around me dissipates. Luke and Dax both come into view.

Luke's sitting in his normal spot at the large table with some papers spread out in front of him while Dax has the hidden wall of weapons open, taking inventory.

"I'm surprised you came so quickly." Luke turns around and arches an eyebrow. "Whenever I ask for you to come here, you usually make sure to take your time."

Of course he would know I was here. He has the same kind of powers as I, so he can feel when I enter the room. I'm getting to where I can sense the same thing, but he has several years of experience over me, and my power is kind of overwhelming me at this point.

"I hate it when you both do that." Dax turns around with a frown. "Normal reapers don't appear out of thin air."

"And normal reapers aren't elders." Luke winks at me and stands.

Yeah, let's not go there right now. I take a step, and a breeze follows, brushing along my body.

"So... how are things?" Luke's brows furrow together.

"Still getting acclimated." There, that's not a lie and opens the door for more conversation. I don't want to just blurt it all out, but I need help.

"Man, this breeze would have come in handy while we were in hell." Dax grins and picks up one of the swords. "But I'm not complaining. Getting to watch a hot girl kick ass was worth it."

For some reason, when he makes comments like that, I want to hide my face. I clear my throat and ignore him.

"Has that been happening a lot?" Luke purses his lips and taps his chin. "The breeze and such?"

"Well..." It's still hard to trust him, but I've decided to, at least for now. "Earlier, a plant grew twice its size in my hand, and I didn't mean for it to happen." I'll leave out the part where I was distracted and kissing Charlie. Some details don't have to be shared, right?

"Hmmmm." He rubs a hand over his face and begins to pace. "So you're not able to control the elements that are linked to you at all times. It's as if they are taking on a life of their own."

He could say that again. I can control them when I fully concentrate, but otherwise, no. He's right. Why haven't I realized that before now?

"What does that mean?" Dax put downs the sword and focuses on me. "Is she all right?"

"Well, we need her to get to the fourth artifact to ensure balance, but until then, I want to test something to see what's going on." Luke's eyes focus on me, and he straightens his shoulders. "Do you mind coming somewhere with me? I have a theory I want to test out."

I'm not sure what to make of that, but at this point, I need to know what's going on, too. "Yeah, sure. But no funny business. If something feels off, I'm leaving." One thing I won't do is put myself in any uncomfortable situations just for the sake of keeping the peace.

"Of course." He places a hand over his heart and nods. "We are on the same team."

That's what he keeps saying. And so far, I haven't seen anything that proves otherwise.

"Stay here and make sure no one snoops around." He turns to Dax and motions to his desk. "We will be back shortly."

"Got it." Dax's stormy eyes meet mine. "Be safe, and stay out of trouble."

Despite what everyone thinks, I don't like to get in trouble. It just seems to find me. But he's very concerned for some reason. "Just worry about yourself. I'll be fine."

Luke grabs my hand, and the air begins to churn around us.

Damn, he wasn't kidding when he said *let's go*. Within seconds, we are transporting to our destination, wherever that is. I've never been there before, so this is another first for me.

As soon as we arrive, the air calms down around us.

When I look around, I realize we're in someone's house. We're right inside the front door, which also happens to be the living room. There's a long, overstuffed couch in front of the window and a rocking chair to the side. On the other side of the room, a TV sits above a fireplace.

Something slams shut from the left side of the house. "I swear this laundry keeps growing. I'm going to be in here folding it all day." An older woman's voice echoes into the living room.

"Please, follow me." Luke turns right toward the hallway. "There is someone you need to see."

My body stiffens, and I bite my bottom lip. "Why don't you bring this person out here? I don't mind waiting."

He pauses and lets out a deep sigh. "Christina, will you please just come on." His shoulders drop, and his voice sounds tired. "I get you're still wary of me, but this person can't make it out here."

"Fine." He's up to something, but I'm not sure what. "I'm assuming it's just us and this other person here?"

"Yes, this person has been sick for a very long time." He opens the door, leading us into the back master bedroom.

There is an older man lying on the bed with an oxygen mask on his face. He's breathing in and out but is in a very deep sleep. His face is sagging, and his skin is turning yellow.

"What's wrong with him?" The stench of death is already upon him, so he doesn't have much longer. It's strange because that smell used to turn my stomach, but now it doesn't faze me at all.

"He's suffered a stroke." Luke stares at the man and frowns. "He hasn't been able to function since. His wife is just down the hall and will be back in just a few moments."

"So... why are we here?" There is always a reason with him.

"Like I said, I want to test something." He nods at the man. "Why don't you heal him?"

"Really?" This will be easy. My healing ability has always been the most natural for me, so it'll be a piece of cake.

"Yes, otherwise he is marked to die tonight." Luke leans back against the wall and grins. "So, if you can heal him, he'll get to live a few more years."

"Okay, one healed old man coming right up." I walk over

to the man on the bed, and my white power churns inside me. As it begins to move, the three elemental powers along with my reaper magic begin to swirl, increasing strength.

I open my hand and touch the old man's chest. As soon as my power connects with his soul, it begins to blend in with it unlike any other time before.

His soul connects with me, and I see flickers of his life and memories. The first time he met his wife, the moments when his son and daughter were born, all of these different moments of time are recalled in my mind as if I'm part of him.

When I reach the end of his life's slide show, it's somehow clear that he has lived his life and it's time for him to die. My white power begins to dim, and my black reaper power begins to strengthen in its stead.

But that's not what I'm supposed to do right now. I'm supposed to be giving him a few more years with his family. The vibrant purple strand of the fire element lights up and flashes inside me and into my mind.

Oh my God. This is what got me in that mess to begin with. Saving this person is not the right thing to do. His time is up, and the balance of the world depends on life and death. Him having a few more years past his due time on Earth with his family is not worth risking the world. It makes me no better than Damien, who collects souls instead of letting them go into their afterlife. I've endangered the world because I saved one person – Becca. I can't do it again.

The strands of the artifacts rush into the reaper powers to form a swirl of black, brown, blue, and purple. Instead of healing, the reaper magic begins working, and my hands begin to suction the soul out of the body.

This man doesn't fight me; he's ready to go home. His

soul comes willingly, and soon he's passing through my body and going into his afterlife.

There is no coldness or nausea this time. When the transition is complete, I open my eyes to find Luke staring at me with his mouth wide open.

"You... You reaped him." His face turns a shade more pale, and he rubs his fingers together.

If he thinks he's the only one surprised, he's got another think coming. "I know, but I had to. Extending his life would cause problems. I saw it."

He shakes his head, and his forehead wrinkles. "What do you mean?"

My magic suddenly flares inside me and takes my breath away. I stumble and almost fall to the floor.

"What's wrong?" Luke rushes over to me and takes my arm. "Are you okay?"

"No..." Another wave of power crashes over me, and it feels as if my insides are going to be ripped to shreds if I don't let it out. It's never been this strong before. "My power..." I can't even finish my sentence because holding it in takes all my concentration. Shit, there is no way I can keep it inside for much longer.

3

H is grip tightens on my arm. "Christina, we have to go. There is still someone in the house. You can't lose control."

My power swirls and presses against my core, threatening to burst right out if I can't control it fast. My knees buckle, and I drop to the floor even with Luke there trying to keep me upright. I'm at the mercy of the artifacts.

"Shit." With his free hand, he pulls out his cell phone and puts it to his ear. "Dax, clear the mansion the best you can. We are coming back now."

I close my eyes, unable to keep them open. I'm going to die right here and now. I'm not even going to get a chance to tell Charlie I love him one last time.

The air begins to churn, whipping around me, increasing the discomfort inside me. At least I won't kill the old lady doing laundry. It'll be hard enough on the family that the old man died. His memories showed a very loving and close family.

Soon, we're back at the mansion, and I curl up in the

fetal position on the floor. I don't know how much longer I have, but each breath hurts.

"What the hell happened?" Dax rushes over and bends down next to me. As soon as he touches my skin, he jerks back. "Ouch. You feel as if you're on fire. What the hell?"

What am I supposed to do? I've got to get out of here.

"You have to calm down." Luke's tone is low, almost soothing. "Take control of the power and push it down. Things are going to get bad if you don't. We need you."

Doesn't he think I know that? If I were feeling better, I would slap him. Everything inside me is quivering against the ferocity of the magic. It wants out and now.

Dax closes his eyes and takes in a deep breath. "We've got to get you out of here, Luke, in case she can't stop it."

Thank God. At least one of them has some common sense.

"What?" Luke's head jerks up, and he glares. "We need her. We can't win without the artifacts."

"Yeah, but if we lose you, who's to say the next two replacements won't go rogue with the oldest Elder?" Dax's voice cracks, but he stands tall. "We need you just as much as we need her, especially if she doesn't make it."

My ears begin ringing from all the pressure. They need to go and now. Dax is right and Luke needs to get on with it.

"Fine." Luke glances at me one last time, concern shining through his eyes. "I hate it, but you're right. Let's go."

Grabbing Luke, Dax pulls them both through the portal he already had open.

Holy crap. I'm alone now, and I need to get out of here. I can't hurt all the people in here. There must be at least ten butlers who are always here, and no telling if there is anyone else in the dungeon or what not.

I roll over to my belly and attempt to get up on my hands and knees but fall back down. Ugh, I've got to find a freaking way out. I won't have my life end in such a catastrophe.

A strong gust of wind blows into the room and picks me up. I'm lifted about five feet in the air.

What the hell is going on?

Something pulls at me, and my body moves toward the windows in the back of Luke's office. I'm not moving slow or fast, but somewhere in between. I'm reminded of long-ago summer days when Beth and I would ride our bikes down the road with no destination in sight. Fast enough to feel a breeze, but we weren't in any rush.

As I get close to the window, the power begins vibrating, and my vision begins to bounce. I can't see straight, but I hear a loud crash and feel piercing cuts all over my body. I've gone right through the window

The smell of fresh cut grass hits my nose, which makes me want to laugh for some reason. I'm losing my damn mind right before I die. I wonder if everyone does or if it's just me. Hell, I'm flying for goodness sake.

I fly through the air and land at the base of a huge oak tree. As soon as my back hits the bark, more power from the ground bleeds into me. My vision goes black, and the pain is like never before. I don't know where I begin or end, and it feels as if I'm splitting in two. The artifacts' energy glows brighter, and soon it rips me apart and pours out of me.

———— • • • ————

"Is she okay?" Dax's tone is hoarse, and then he coughs.

"Yeah, at least for now she is." Luke is right beside me, and a hand brushes some hair off of my face.

My eyelids flutter, but I still can't open them. What is going on? How am I still alive? My body feels heavy, and my breathing is shallow.

"I can't believe she did all this." Dax laughs and then stops short. "I mean, she's something, but this is scary. She doesn't deserve this."

"Don't you think I know this?" Luke huffs, and his hand leaves my face. "However, it wasn't my choice. I didn't choose her for this."

Wow, they sound like they really believe in me. Good thing I don't need validation any longer. I can do this with or without their support. I tug at the white power inside me, and it unfurls and begins circulating through me. As soon as it's made a round through my body, I can breathe easier, and the pain isn't quite as bad.

I've never tried healing myself before, but hey, at least it worked. This time, my eyes open, and I find Luke kneeling over me.

"How bad do you hurt?" His suit is in disarray, and there is dust all over his jacket.

I take a deep breath, letting air fill my lungs. "Actually, I'm okay. I don't know how, but I'm fine." My throat is dry, grainy, and I cough. I need water or something to drink. I begin to sit up when Dax comes to my other side and places a hand on my arm.

"Take a minute before getting up. Make sure you have your bearings." He licks his lips and shakes his head. "You went through a huge ordeal."

"You don't think I know that? I was the one living through it." Times like these make me hate being around people. They act like I'm not part of what's going on, like I'm just a bystander.

A small grin spreads across his face. "I think she's going to be just fine. There's my fire cracker."

Where did this nickname come from all of a sudden? It's sweet but makes me feel a little uncomfortable. It's almost like he's turning into a different person. That's how Becca started out too.

"Can you both just focus for a minute?" Luke rolls his eyes, and he glances behind him. "How in the world did you get out here? We left you in my office."

Hell, he's right. Everything comes back to me. "I didn't want to injure anyone. I remember focusing on that. Those butlers are just doing their jobs. Many probably would rather be doing something else. So I wanted to make sure everyone was safe, and somehow a major wind gust picked me up and brought me out here."

"Did you come out the window?" Luke frowns and glances at my arms. "One is broken but I don't see any cuts."

"Yeah, I did." That part is hazy, but I do remember the crash and pain. "But I'm sure my healing power fixed or did other things to cover the injuries up." I sit up, wanting to see what they keep looking around at, but I'm not prepared for what I see.

The wind had taken me a good two hundred yards from the house, and everything even up to the mansion is charred or crumbled. The brown stone on the back side of the mansion now crumbles and falls to the ground, and the windows are cracked.

The ground is churned and broken as if an earthquake happened. All the grass is now gone. The large trees that covered the property for privacy are flattened as if they were never there to begin with. The only proof of them are the wide tree stumps that rise slightly out of the ground.

Shit, even the tree I was laying under is gone. What did I do? How is it possible that I caused this much destruction when I wasn't even aware? "I... I did this?"

"Yes, but don't worry. We can fix it in no time." Luke steps in front of me.

"Did I hurt anyone?" Oh, God. I messed up the side of the house, which means I could have killed someone.

"Only minor injuries." Dax places a hand on my shoulder and comes up beside me. "Nothing major at all. I think the worst one was a twisted ankle."

Why does that not make me feel better? I mean, I'm glad I didn't kill someone, but I still hurt someone. "What if this happens again? I might not be so lucky again."

"You were so worried that you somehow managed to get yourself out here, saving a dozen people." Luke lowers his head and stares me dead in the eye. "You have more control over yourself than you give yourself credit for. You're stronger than you realize."

He's right. I managed to save myself and not destroy too much stuff at one time. That's a win within itself.

"But you do realize this is going to continue to get worse until you find the fourth artifact." Luke arches an eyebrow and crosses his arm. "This will be a pleasant memory if things don't happen fast."

As if responding to his statement, the powers inside me begin to collide with one another. Very similar to what they did before I got the Flame of Hell. "You're right. Things aren't feeling right again."

"Wait... This is going to happen again?" Dax frowns, and his body tenses.

"Yes, if we don't work fast." Luke glances at him and then back to me. "But it's the last one. Then, all four elements will be in your control and, thus, balanced. You won't have to worry about any of this again."

No matter how much I wish he was wrong, he's not. I must get to the fourth artifact and fast. I need the balance, or otherwise I'll implode just like the witch told me before I left to get the Flame from Hell. It's now or never.

4

My throat feels as if it's been ripped apart by a sandblaster. In my mass of chaos, I swallowed a lot of dirt. "Then we need to..." I begin coughing and can't finish my sentence.

Dax frowns. "She needs water."

"Let's go back inside and get her something to drink while we figure out where this last element is." Luke grabs my arm lightly and tugs me toward the house.

I haven't told them that the artifact has been found, but in my defense, it hasn't come up. Between getting on the council and acclimating to my powers, this last week has been a whirlwind.

We walk around the debris and past the door that is partially ajar. Crap, I messed this place up.

"Don't worry about this." Luke motions to the side of the house. "This will be fixed in no time. Probably by the end of the day. We already have the emergency crew on the way."

Of course they do; the council couldn't have their mansion imperfect for long.

He leads us a little further down where there is another

door. This section of the place is still intact except that the grass is a shade of light brown. He opens the door and motions us in. "Go on into my office and have her sit down. I'll go get some water for her. The butlers are preoccupied right now."

"I bet they are." Dax murmurs close to my ear.

If I weren't so uncomfortable, I'd snort, but I just stopped coughing not too long ago. "Let's just go." I head on in, not waiting for him at all.

As soon as I enter the room, I sit down on the couch in the corner. It's not the most comfortable seat in the world, but it'll do. The fabric is stiff since no one uses it and it's not broken in, but I'm still a little worn out from my accident.

"So are you really okay?" Dax stands in front of me and crosses his arms.

Dear God, my hand itches to smack him. "Yeah, I'm fine. We've been through Hell before, so it's not like this is much different."

"In Hell, you didn't almost implode." Dax's jaw twitches, and his tone lowers.

"The best thing to prevent it from happening again is to get the fourth artifact." I don't like how he pays attention to me half the time. We're friends, but there are times where it feels off. Is he developing deeper feelings for me?

"Now that is true." He drops his arms and runs a hand along the back of his neck. "Do you have any idea where it is? Don't you normally see it?"

"Yeah, it's in a weird world." Whenever I see the artifact, it's just three floaty circles, but it's surrounded by water. "It's mainly water."

The door opens, and Luke walks in with a large glass. "Here you go." He hands it to me and smiles. "Drink up."

Not wasting any time, I grab it from him and take a big

sip. The cool water hits the back of my parched throat, and it hurts for a brief second before it brings relief. I drink it so fast that water spills out of my mouth and drips down my chin.

"Whoa there, firecracker." Dax laughs. "You're going to spill more than you drink."

When the glass is empty, I lower it and hand it back to Luke. "Thanks."

His eyes widen, and his mouth opens and closes.

"So, are you both ready to go get the artifact?" We don't have any time to waste, and I'm worried that I could lose control again any second.

"Of course." Luke closes his mouth and sets the glass down on the table. "Let's get there and get back."

Dax steps over to me and touches both mine and Luke's arm. "I'm ready when you are."

I close my eyes so I can picture the world perfectly. I need to make sure we land in just the right location. What comes to mind is a place where there is emerald blue water everywhere. I can't see land in any direction. "You both need to be prepared to swim." Before they can ask any questions, I project the image out to Dax, ready for him to take us there.

"Wow, you weren't kidding when you said it's a water world." Dax takes in a deep breath, and then he removes his hand from Luke to draw the portal. "Shit."

"Christina, are you projecting the image still?" Luke's voice is puzzled.

"Yeah." I open my eyes and see that Dax's portal isn't working. "What the hell?"

"I... I don't know." Dax shakes his head. "Maybe I'm the tired one this time."

That could be true. The first time in Hell, I couldn't locate the Flame because I was too tired from everything else. My abilities weren't working right. His could be the same way.

A loud knock at the door startles me. A butler joins us, his face red from exertion or embarrassment. I'm not sure. "Good afternoon. The Elder Couple has requested the presence of the two of you." He points at Luke and me. "They request a full council to discuss what happened here earlier today."

Oh great, now I have to see them and act like an Elder.

"We will be right there." Luke nods and grins. "Are they in the meeting room here?"

"Yes, they are there waiting on you both." The butler bows and scurries out of the room.

That's so stupid. They shouldn't be bowing to us. Hell, they are part reapers after all.

"Do I need to go with you two?" Dax is frowning and popping his knuckles.

"No, that would cause more trouble than it's worth." Luke focuses on me and nods to the door. "Come on. We better get moving. They get ornery if they have to wait."

"Sounds like someone else I know." I roll my eyes and smile. "And don't worry, Dax. I can take them."

"I'm sure you can." He chuckles as we leave the room.

All too soon, we enter the same room where the council threatened me not even three months ago. The Elder couple are standing on the side of the room, deep in conversation.

Today, the lady has her gray hair in her typical updo. She's wrapped an arm around her waist, making the long lavender blue dress bunch.

The man is shaking his head and tugging at his black suit jacket. Whatever they're discussing, they seem to be riled up.

"Well, good afternoon." Luke's voice is charismatic, and he smiles at them like they are good friends.

They both smile at him, but when their eyes turn to me, the smiles fall from their faces.

"You." The lady points at me, and her voices quivers. "You've been a member of this council for a short time, and you've already messed up our Mansion."

Why did they even agree to allow me on the council? Luke still won't tell me the answer to that one. "No big deal. I hear the emergency crew is on the way. If you threaten the right people, no one will ever find out what happened."

"Christina." Luke's tone is chastising, but I can see the humor in his eyes. "Even if you are part of this council right now, it is temporary. You should remember that and be nice."

"You, little girl, need to learn respect." The Elder man looks down his nose at me. "Even if you have similar powers as we do, we can still squash you." Even as he says the words, the elements around him attempt to jerk away from him. Almost as if they are afraid of him touching them.

Opening up my senses, I connect to the air and earth in the room. Even though the elements don't speak, I can tell how they are feeling, and right now, they can sense how desperate this couple is to control them.

"I don't understand how she could be the one able to control these strong artifacts." The lady wrinkles her nose and glares. "Someone of my caliber should be that person."

Oh, hell no. I'm tired of how she cuts me down. "See, that's where..."

Luke grabs my arm and squeezes hard. "That may be true, but the fact remains, if we want the power of the artifacts on our side, then she is part of us."

Dammit, he's trying to be reasonable, but I just want to smack her.

"Not if she doesn't get the fourth one." The lady arches an eyebrow and gives me a menacing smile.

Nice, she *wants* me to implode. I'll make sure she's standing right beside me.

"Well, the witch came to visit her before we left for Hell." Luke frowns and pulls me closer to her. "She knows how to disperse the artifacts back to their original places."

"What?" The elder man clenches his hands. "I thought..."

The lady raises a hand and hisses. "Shush."

Is this why Luke has been nice to me? He's playing this part a little too well right now.

"This has been very problematic, and now you can see why we are in the situation we're in." Luke drops his hand from my arm and runs a hand down his face. "Unfortunately, we need her to get the fourth artifact and fast. Otherwise, the life we know is over."

"Fine." The lady paces the area in front of us. "You can use our resources to find a way to get her there, but I want her back here to me as soon as it's done."

Does she think I will come back here to her when it's all said and done? I bite my tongue to keep from laughing. "Don't worry about it. I don't need your help."

"Christina..." Luke narrows his eyes at me.

Oh, no. His little act here as made me doubt him more. "I don't trust any of you."

"It doesn't matter if you trust us." The lady lifts her head high and snarls. "You will take our help and come back to us so we can save the world."

"Actually, you're going to all stay away from me and leave me to my own devices." I'll be damned if I take another resource from them.

"Like hell." The lady stomps her way over to me and stabs a finger into my chest. "If you don't stop this nonsense, your parents and lover boy will pay the price for your disobedience."

I grab her finger and twist it. She yelps and tries to tug away, but I hold firm. "No, you won't do a damn thing to any of them. If you do, I'll make sure your life is a living hell." I smirk and let my hatred bubble up. "After all, I do have Hell's Flame burning inside me. Would you all like to feel?" My power begins to flare inside me, and I let a little flow through me.

She whimpers and yanks her finger away harder. "Stop, that hurts."

"If you think that hurts," I say as I let her go and take a step into her personal space, "if you or anyone else lays a hand on anyone I care about, imagine what happened outside today focused on you."

Her face turns a shade of white I've never seen on her before, and the elder man's mouth is dropped open. I turn on my heels and walk out the door. I don't bother to look at Luke.

I close my eyes and focus on my apartment. Within seconds, I've transported myself there. When the room comes into view, Charlie is sitting down on my couch, reading a book.

His blond hair is messy from his day at work, and his lips are pursed over whatever section he's reading.

"Hey there." It seems like it's been forever since I've seen him, but in reality, it's only been a few hours.

He tosses the book on the couch and stands. "Hey, what happened today? Something felt off, and I came straight here." He takes a few steps and pulls me into his arm.

"It was a crap day." I fill him in on everything and bury my face into his chest. I'm so glad I have him.

"Oh, sweetheart." He leans back and brushes his fingers across my face. "We're going to figure this out. Nothing bad is going to happen to you. It can't. I love you so damn much."

How I wish that was true. Once upon a time, I did think it. Hell, it was only four months ago that I thought if I succeeded and somehow obtained my parent's love, everything would be okay. Shit, I wish I could be that naive girl again. But those days are long gone, and I'm not even sure I'm going to make it out of this alive.

5

As I wake up the next morning, I can feel that my body and mind are well-rested once again. I hadn't even realized how much my little episode took out of me yesterday. It's kind of scary what took place, and it's going to continue to get worse if I don't get the Water Artifact and soon.

An arm wraps around me and pulls me against a warm firm chest. "Hey, beautiful."

I'm so glad Charlie stayed with me last night. I needed him. I snuggle into him and grin. "Hey, yourself."

He lifts his head and peppers my neck with kisses. "I'm not done with you yet. You can't leave."

My heart speeds up in my chest, and I giggle. "I don't want to, but there is some stuff I have to do." It's so hard to say those words, but every minute I lay here is another second closer to a meltdown.

His lips are still on my neck. "Exactly what all do you have planned?" His arm stiffens around me, and his breathing picks up.

He already assumes I'm going without him. But after last

night, I can't leave him behind again. Time and time again, he's proven we're stronger together than apart. "Well, I was hoping that you're up for some traveling."

"What does that mean?" He sits up and looks down at my face. "What are you asking me?" He tilts his head, his hazel eyes guarded.

"I think it was my fault that we couldn't get to the water world yesterday. I was worn out like I was in Hell when I couldn't locate the Flame." All along, we thought Dax was the problem, but now I'm sure it was me. "I'm positive that with Dax, I can get there now."

He shakes his head and huffs. "So... you're leaving again." He runs a hand through his hair. "At least I should be happy that you're telling me ahead of time."

"That's not fair at all." Did he not hear me earlier? "Don't make me take back what I said. I thought you going would make me stronger, but if you're going to bicker with me, then maybe it's a bad idea."

"You referenced you and Dax going; not me." He points at me and narrows his eyes. "I thought at first you were going that direction, but that last sentence seems to take it away. In my defense, what am I to think based on your history?"

"I get it, but why don't you ask before just assuming the worst?" He does have a point, but I'm not going to take all of the blame. "So yes, I was hoping you might want to join us this time."

"Hell yeah, I do." He places his arms on both sides of me, trapping me in. "For once, it would be nice not to be worried sick the entire time you're gone."

"It's not that it's ever been on purpose." Things always seem to happen outside of my control. "This time, I want to be ahead of the game with us dictating who's going and when." It also doesn't hurt knowing I have three artifacts running inside me and that I can protect him.

A smile fills his face. "I am onboard with that suggestion, and you're right. We need to get moving before something bad happens. But first..." He leans down and kisses me, leaving me breathless.

I enjoy the moment but then pull away. There is no telling when my powers will get screwy again. "I hate to do this, but I'm going to get up and take a quick shower."

"Yeah, okay." He lifts his arms and gets out of the bed. "While you're getting ready, I'll get dressed and grab some things to eat on the way. I'm assuming Dax is at the Mansion."

"That's where he should be, but I'll locate him before we go." I grab some clean clothes and head into the bathroom. "I should only be a few minutes."

Within five minutes, I'm out of the shower and slipping on my blue jeans and tank top. It may not be the most comfortable for some people, but this is what I like to wear. I put my hair into a ponytail and then brush my teeth. When it's all said and done, I walk out and find Charlie stuffing food and water into a backpack.

He's dressed in jeans as well and a fitted shirt that shows off his lean, muscular chest. He glances at me and licks his lips. "I wish we weren't rushing off."

Me too. And to think I had that body draped over me last night. A repeat sure would be nice this morning. "We'll make sure to make up for lost time when we get back."

A loud knock at the door echoes between us.

"Are you expecting someone?" Charlie glances at the door and back at me.

"No." It's still early in the morning, so I have no clue who would be here at this hour.

"Hey." Dax smiles as I open the door. His eyes search the room behind me; as soon as they land on Charlie, the smile disappears. "Oh, I didn't realize you had company."

The air around him seems a little off today; there is a hint of light gray in his aura. That's odd. "I wouldn't say he was company. He's practically here as much as I am."

Charlie steps up beside me and wraps an arm around my waist. "That's a very true statement. I mean, I even sleep over almost every night."

Oh my God. Did he go there? Granted, I get that Dax puts off a weird vibe sometimes, but that's pretty much proclaiming we have sex without saying those three little letters out loud.

Dax winces and clears his throat. "Ummm... Sorry I interrupted, but something felt off. I had to come over and check on you."

Something doesn't add up. "Is the council watching me or something?"

"What?" HIs mouth drops open, and he shakes his head. "No."

"Really?" Charlie's arm tightens around me, and he lifts his chin. "We were about to leave to find you, and all of a sudden, you're at our door."

"You guys were coming to find me?" Dax focuses back on me. "Are you okay?"

If one more person asks me that, I might scream. "Yeah, but how did you know to come here. It does sound fishy."

"Hell, Chris." Dax throws up both hands. "You're one of the council members now. They can't watch you like they used to, or it would look bad."

"Don't be fooled. They don't trust me." The elder lady would throw me back in the dungeon if she could.

"I didn't say they trusted you." He drops his hands again

and sighs. "Only that they can't watch you like they used to. They have to save face."

"I don't know." Charlie looks down at me. "His timing is really suspect."

"Look." Dax steps into the apartment and into my personal space. "I had a feeling earlier that woke me up and sensed you needed me for some reason. I'm not sure why, but I couldn't shake it. That's the only reason why I'm here."

"Chris..." Charlie's tone is low.

Yeah, I get he doesn't trust Dax, but in all fairness, he doesn't know him. I take in Dax's stormy gray eyes and search for something. I'm not sure what, but the elements inside me do.

He stands tall, letting me search for whatever it is I need. "I'm not going anywhere, so take your time."

It takes a moment, but something inside me stirs. Whether Charlie likes it or not, Dax is someone I can trust. I'm not sure how I know it, but I do. My instincts haven't let me down yet, so I'm going to trust them. "Fine, but only the essential information makes it back to Luke and the others." This is what I need to confirm. Dax is loyal to Luke, but at the end of the day, everything inside of me tells me he'll do what's right.

"Are you sure?" Charlie whispers in my ear.

"I trust him." I turn to Charlie and give him a small smile. "But this time, you'll be there to watch my back."

"Of course I won't run and tell them anything they don't have to know." Dax sighs and rubs the back of his neck. "Yes, I'm loyal to Luke but to you as well. You've saved my life more than once."

"Good. That's what I was hoping you'd say." It's now time to get moving. Time is running out, and I don't want to have any more accidents. "If that's the case, are you ready to head on to that water realm?"

"Oh, is that why you were coming to look for me?" He bites his lip and taps his foot. "I'm still not sure if I can get us there. I haven't figured out what the problem was yesterday."

"I'm pretty sure it was me." In fact, I'm positive. Yesterday was kind of crazy. "I was exhausted just like that time in Hell."

"Why didn't you say anything?" Dax's forehead wrinkles and he takes a step closer to me.

"Because you guys always push her." Charlie scowls at him and takes my hand. "If you all would let her breathe, it would be best for everyone."

"Hey, I went down there to protect her." Dax's nostrils flare.

"Guys, quit it." Dear God, this is ridiculous. "It wasn't Dax's fault we went to Hell. It was Luke's, but that's just because he knows I'm on a time crunch." I point to Charlie then Dax. "Both of you need to get along, or this trip is going to end in disaster."

"Wait." Dax's eyes widen. "Is he going with us?"

"Damn right I am." Charlie growls and puffs up his chest.

Dax is clearly not pleased over Charlie's coming. "Stop it. Enough." I don't understand why Dax is acting this way, and Charlie is practically peeing all over me. Neither have acted this irrational before. "Yeah, Charlie is going to go with us this time. I'm not leaving him behind. Do you have a problem with it?"

It takes a few seconds, but Dax finally lets out a deep breath. "No, let's get this thing on the road."

I can't agree more. "Charlie, I'm going to imagine the place, and then Dax is going to take us there. Be ready for it."

"Got it." Charlie tightens his grip on my hand. "I'm ready when you are."

I close my eyes and focus on the fourth artifact. The three round circles of water that float in the air appear in my mind. When I pull back to see the location again, I see water surrounding it, but it's in a protected area on a stretch of dry land. The water is reflecting some of the barriers, so I can't make out exactly how it's being held. Once I have the artifact locked and loaded in my mind, I project it out to Dax.

Dax grabs my hand and touches Charlie's arm, and soon we are teleporting to this new world. I'm not sure where we will land, but hopefully we can just grab the artifact and head back within minutes.

When we appear in the water world, my feet sink into knee deep, brown, crusty water. "What the hell?"

I take a look around, and see that there are low hanging trees everywhere and brown, swampy water all around us. It smells bad, and I'm holding in a gag. This isn't what I saw when I pictured the Water Artifact.

"Uh... babe." Charlie turns to me, making a splash. "Where is this artifact?"

"I have no clue." I glance at Dax. "Is that the image you saw when I projected it out?"

He shakes his head no.

Great, that's not what I saw either. We are nowhere near the freaking artifact but, instead, in the middle of a swamp.

6

Crap, I hope we are at least in the right realm. I glance up at the sky and blink twice. "Is that two suns?" Granted, neither one is as bright as the one back home, but together they light up the entire sky.

Charlie lifts his head and gasps. "Holy crap, yeah, it is. I've never seen anything like that."

"We're in a different world. Things aren't going to be the same." Dax is glancing around on high alert.

That's very true. Every world we've gone to has been different. For some reason, I expected this one to be more similar. Between all of the water and two suns, I'm not sure there is any land to be found. The water is a similar color and feel, and the trees are the same shade but larger. "Okay, true. But for some reason, that caught me off guard."

"We need to get out of this water." Charlie takes a few steps my direction and searches in the water. "There is no telling what's hidden in here with us."

Shit, I hadn't even thought of that. "Well, unless you want to go back, I don't see a way around it now."

Dax's tone is low, and his body tenses. "We need to get

out of this and fast. Can you get a read on the artifact so we know which way to head?"

They're right. I need to focus. "Let me try now." I close my eyes and try to block out everything around me. Something is throwing us off, and I need to limit my distractions.

The image of the three bubbles pops up in my head, but as soon as it does, it's reflected multiple times almost like one of those fun house mirrors at an amusement park. I can't even see the water around it like I did back on Earth. What the hell is going on?

I can't give up. We've got to find this. My time is running out, and this must be the right place. I try to focus on the center image, but the mirror images flash, causing me to break my focus. Dammit, this isn't going to work. I hate to admit failure, but they need to know. "I can't get the location. I'm sorry."

A hand touches my shoulder, and lips press against my forehead. "You've done your best. We'll figure it out. We're in this together."

Oh, thank God he's here. Growing up, he may have given me hell, but he's always been honest with me. I trust him in a way that no one can touch. Charlie always seems to know how to comfort me even before I'm aware that I need comforting. "Yeah, but if we can't find it, I'm screwed."

"We've been here before." Dax frowns and shakes his head. "We got through it then, and we'll figure it out now."

Something like the roar of an engine fills the air. All three of us turn our heads in the direction of the sound, and soon three cargo planes that resemble the military ones back on Earth fill the sky. They fly directly over us and head to the west.

"Bingo." Charlie lets out a breath. "Let's follow them. They have to be heading somewhere they can land."

That's true. Once we get out of this water, maybe we can find help.

"Let's go. I don't want to be stuck out here at night." Dax splashes off in the direction of the planes.

Charlie intertwines his fingers with mine and tugs me after him. "Come on. We all need to stay together."

Progress is slow, especially since we're keeping an eye out for anything that could attack us. I fully expect an alligator to pop up at any second, but who knows if they even exist on this planet.

After a while, I realize that the guys have flanked me, one on each side, as we wade. I want to say something, but I bite my tongue. Maybe they didn't do it on purpose. I mean, they both know me and not each other. It could have just happened like that, right?

Just as I'm about to give up and head home, the murky water clears and gets deeper, and I can see some immense areas that are designed to hold water up ahead.

In front of us, tall grass breaks through the water, but other than that, the water stands still. It's marked off in sections to the left and right with a wide flowing section of water in the middle as if for traveling.

"Hey, look." Charlie points to a large tree where the swamp ends and meets the clear water.

There is a boat tied off there. It's not huge, but hell, it's dry. "Well, it has to be someone's." I glance around, but there's no one in sight. That's freaking weird.

"It's ours now." Dax splashes over to it and sighs. "I hate to do it, but we are running out of time, and we need to get to wherever those planes went. There is no telling how far it is, and this water is getting deeper."

He's right again. I hate stealing but as the angel told me in the Angel Realm, sometimes we must make sacrifices for the greater good. "Fine. Let's just do it. I don't know how much longer I can go like this anyway."

"We're making the right call." Charlie squeezes my hand. "We'll try to bring it back when it's all said and done."

Yeah, that's wishful thinking. We'll be heading right back to Earth when it's all said and done. "Let's just go."

We swim to the small wooden boat with three sections for seats, and Dax climbs in first, causing the boat to rock back and forth. He slips and lands on his back in the middle section. "Shit, that hurts."

A giggle escapes me. "Oh suck it up. You've been stabbed before."

He cuts his eyes at me and grins. "Yeah, but let me just have this moment." He sits and then holds his hand out to me. "Charlie, can you help me boost her up?"

What the hell? I can get myself into that boat. I open my mouth to complain, but Charlie beats me by grabbing my waist and hoisting me up in the air.

Dax wraps his arm around me and pulls me into the front of the boat. "Stay here and try not to cause trouble." He grabs Charlie's arm, helping him in as well.

I don't know what all the fuss was about at the apartment, but they're playing nice now. Seeing them work together eases some of my worry.

All right, let's get moving. "Are we ready to go?" I turn to face them, feeling my clothes cling to me. Ugh, I hate wet clothes. Tapping into my power, I channel the wind to blow through the boat and dry our clothes. It's an intense breeze, but I'm prepared.

"Whoa." Charlie and Dax grab onto the side of the boat as the wind hits us.

However, it doesn't last long because we're dried in

seconds. "Oh, thank God. I couldn't take being wet another second."

"You didn't think to warn us?" Charlie grins at me and shakes his head.

"Yeah, really." Dax's shoulders tense, and his eyes narrow. "That could have tipped us over."

Wow, I'm getting some serious anger vibes from Dax right now. "Yeah, I guess I should've, but I didn't think about it."

"You never think, do you?" He tilts his head, and the air around him turns that slight gray hue once more.

Oh, hell no. "Actually, I think a lot. Weren't you the one who got stabbed in Hell and almost died?" He's never acted like this before, so I'm not sure what his problem is.

"She didn't do anything wrong. Don't get your panties in a wad." Charlie picks up an oar and hands it to Dax. "Let's get moving. We have an artifact to find."

Taking the oar, Dax relaxes his shoulders and breathes in. "Yeah, you're right. I don't know what just came over me." He glances at me and puts his oar in the water. "I'm sorry. That was uncalled for."

Yeah, I'm not going to tell him it's okay because it's not. I hadn't meant to be a jerk to them and he overreacted. I turn forward and remove the rope from the tree branch. We need to get going and fast. There's no telling if someone is close by.

Silence descends over the boat as both guys paddle us down the canal. After leaving the swamp, there is nothing but water farm after water farm as far as the eye can see. I'm not sure how long we've been traveling, but I'm so thankful we've got this boat now. I can't imagine if we had tried to swim this entire way. We wouldn't have made it.

I stare out in front of me, willing for something to

appear beside an endless vista of liquid. A dot suddenly appears ahead, and I keep my eyes on it for a minute, watching it grow bigger. Great, I've been imagining it so hard that I'm beginning to see things. "Guys, I'm losing it."

"What?" Dax stops rowing for a moment and leans forward. "Is it your powers?"

Dear God. "No, but I think I'm seeing things." I point out in front of me to where the dot seems to have gotten even a little bigger. "Is that something besides water up there?"

He lets out a breath and nods. "Yeah, it sure is. It looks like there is an island or something."

"It's about damn time." Charlie grumbles and stretches out his arms. "I'm not sure how much longer I could go on. I was beginning to wonder if there was ever going to be any land."

"It's strange though." I glance curiously around at the endless water. "It looks like this place is surrounded by these farms. Back on Earth we have some variety, but not here."

"You're right." Dax nods and picks up the oars. "But we haven't seen the whole world, or, at least I don't think we have."

It doesn't matter because seeing our destination has re-engerized us. The guys begin rowing faster, and the land gets bigger.

As we get closer, tall buildings come into view as well as machinery that seems to be pumping water out of the reservoirs and into what looks like a huge manufacturing plant. There is condensation blowing out from the top of a large building as the water is run through some type of process.

To the right, there is a long pier that has places for a boat to dock. There are several openings, and we begin to head in that direction.

"Do you think it's smart that we are just walking in here

unannounced?" I don't know why, but I'm kind of nervous. These types of things never end well for me.

"It'll be fine." Charlie grins from behind Dax. "It's not like we have much of a choice anyway."

I hate to agree, but he does have a point.

"Yeah, we'll be fine." Dax points forward. "It's not like we have a choice now. Someone is heading our way."

A man who looks just like us walks in our direction as we pull into the dock and tie off. He's around six feet and appears to be in his mid-forties. He adjusts his blazer jacket as he gets close and straightens his shoulders. He comes off as one of those political types from back home, similar to those on the council.

That sucks for him. I really dislike the council. I climb out of the boat and already feel my feathers ruffle.

Dax and Charlie get out and flank me on each side.

"Well, hello there." The man smiles, and his teeth are so white they are almost blinding. "Welcome to Golden Cascades. I've never seen you before, so I assume it's your first time here. My name is Tide, and I am here to help you. Is there anything in particular you are after?"

A strange feeling overcomes me in that moment, and the three artifacts inside me begin thrumming and reaching out. It's like I'm being pulled past him and into the city. Something is calling me, but I can't get an exact read. I think it's the Water Artifact. It's here and close, yet it's not.

When I focus on the tugging sensation, I realize I can't focus on one solid direction. It's as if it's all over the city and being reflected in my mind. I don't have time for this. I need to find it and fast. "We are after something. It's an artifact that's made of three individual water bubbles."

Charlie looks down at me and raises an eyebrow.

Yeah, maybe that's not the smartest to say. But in all fairness, he asked, and we're low on time.

"Three individual water bubbles?" He laughs loud and adjusts his collar. "I have no idea what you're talking about. Water doesn't stay separated; it merges together."

Oh, wow. He's a condescending asshole. Why am I not surprised?

"Not when they're artifacts." Dax tilts his head and looks him over.

"Uhhh... I guess." Tide clears his throat and glances at Charlie. "You can get a cleansing spell if your stomach is upset, an age-defying spell if you want to stay young." He looks at me and then Dax. "A strength and quickness spell to aid in fights. There are all kinds of spells you can find throughout the market. If you can just give me what you're looking for, I can lead you in the right direction."

He's acting shifty, and I'd bet almost anything that he knows exactly what I'm talking about. "I'm here for the Water Artifact, not any spells. We can do this the nice way or hard way. Which do you prefer?"

Both guys step closer to me, and we face Tide together.

7

Tide arches an eyebrow at me and crosses his arms. "Once again, I have no clue what you're talking about, and to come to a new place and threaten isn't very wise."

The artifacts within me are beginning to pulse. They sense the fourth one close by, and it's causing them to activate. My reaper and healing powers attempt to tug away from the elemental powers, wanting to hide my core. "I can sense it's here." I take a step toward him and try to hide the chaos that's going on inside. "I just need you to tell me where it is instead of playing this game. I've done this way too many times to count, and I don't have time for it now."

Charlie takes a step close to me and places a hand on the small of my back. "She's literally been to Hell and back, so I wouldn't test her."

Shit, he's concerned about me. He knows me too well.

"She *does* know if the artifact is here." Dax scowls at the man and takes a step toward him.

"Well, in this case, I'm afraid she is mistaken." Tide

smooths out his forehead and drops his arm. "I'm sure there might be some type of spell she can find in the market that can get water to do something similar to what she's needing. I just don't know of anything like that off the top of my head."

He's full of it. "Where do you recommend not going?" Maybe that's being sly?

Dax looks at me from the corner of his eyes, and Charlie's shoulders shake a little.

Okay, maybe that wasn't as cool as I'd hoped.

Tide rolls his eyes and shakes his head. "Just go down the pier and in between those two large buildings." He motions to the manufacturing building on the right and a massive glass building on the left. "Once you get past them, the path will open up to a plaza where there are hundreds of tables set up. Each one is selling water spells, and they are congregated in spell types."

My hearing goes out even though his mouth continues running. The artifact powers are now ramming my insides. The pull from the Water Artifact is now attacking me from the outside while the other three are clawing at me from the inside. I can't take it much more of it.

The wind picks up around us, and the ground shakes underneath our feet. I try to rein it in, but it doesn't work. Between the water on the outside and the other artifacts on the inside, it's like I'm trying to contain a tornado.

"What the hell is going on?" Tide's mouth drops open, and his eyes widen.

"It's that artifact you supposedly don't have." Dax's tone is gruff, and he points a finger at him. "That's what's going on."

Charlie takes a step toward me, but I shake my head.

I want to bury myself in his arms, but I refuse to be a weak person any longer. If I'm to handle all four artifacts, I better damn well act like it. I concentrate deep inside me and focus all of my attention there. I push the strands of brown, blue, and purple down and am surprised when they listen. When the ground stops quaking and the wind becomes a breeze, I turn my attention to Tide. "That's just a taste of what I can do."

He pulls at the collar on his shirt and then wipes the sweat off of his forehead. "Fine, you need to go see Ria. She's the keeper of the Water Artifact."

Now we're getting somewhere. "Funny how your tune is changing."

"This isn't my fight." He takes a few more steps back away from me. "Just go through the market area to the last tent on the right. You will find her." He then turns and walks away.

"Hey, are you okay?" Charlie's tone is husky, and his hazel eyes are filled with concern.

"No, I'm not, but we don't have time to spend on this." My power is already clawing to get out again. "We need to find the fourth artifact and fast."

"Let's get moving." Dax heads off in front and glances around. "I don't trust that guy."

At least I'm not the only one getting that vibe.

We move in the direction of the buildings. They look just like the ones on Earth. The manufacturing plant has a giant pump that is sucking water out of the reservoirs and running it through some kind of process. The building across is made of glass, and we can see our reflection in it as we walk by. It's almost as if we are the only ones here, but we know that's not true.

With every step closer to this market, the Water Artifact's hold over me grows stronger. Not able to hold it down any longer, I feel the artifacts' power spring free and attack me once again. I don't want to alert the guys to this, but I'm not sure how much longer I have until I lose it.

Dax is still leading with Charlie right behind him. We emerge from between the two buildings and come to an expansive common area where lush grass covers the ground. There are small wooden tables set up along the sides and a walkway down the middle. There have to be hundreds of tables and people standing side by side.

A lady at one of the tables stands and holds out a small jar of water. "This water can heal your soul. I've spelled it so any ailments will be alleviated at the first drop that passes your lips." She takes a few steps toward us and stares at me. "I'm sure your friend could use it. In return, I would just want a lock of her hair."

Oh, hell no. I want to open my mouth, but all concentration is around my power.

"No, that won't be happening." As if Charlie reads my thoughts, he steps in between us and glares at her. "But thanks for the offer."

It's not like that water would work anyway. I'm not injured in the way she thinks; the energy inside and outside is just too much. The wind picks up, and at this point, it's a losing a battle.

"Holy crap." Dax mumbles, and there is some shuffling. "Back away from her now, and Charlie, do something." His tone is anxious, and there is a hint of panic.

He knows what's going on. He's been around me enough to know when I'm about to melt down.

Hands slide over my cheeks and lift my face up. "Hey, I'm right here." Charlie's tone is soft and soothing.

The pain is so intense inside that I can't open my eyes.

I'm afraid if I blink even once, the release will happen faster, and I don't want to hurt all of these people. It feels as if I'm about to shatter into a million pieces from the pressure building inside of me.

"How can I help you?" He pulls me into his arms and wraps them around me.

No, I can't hurt him. He'll be hurt standing this close to me. The ground begins to shake, and there is a shriek. I pull away hard, but he holds on to me tightly.

"I'm staying here with you." His tone is hard, determined. "Where you go, I go." He begins to run his fingers through my hair and presses a kiss to my forehead.

My heart calms, and my power doesn't seem quite as overwhelming. The ground stops shaking, but the wind still blows hard.

Something crashes at one of the stands, and a lady yelps. "That was one of my best spells."

"Everyone calm down and stand back." A loud, strong woman's voice echoes against the clearing. "There is no reason for alarm."

"Where the hell do you think you're going?" Dax's tone is low, almost a growl.

Oh, no. What's going on? I'm going to have to suck it up and leave the safety of Charlie's arms. I take a deep breath and look in their direction.

"I'm going to talk to her." The lady's teal blue hair whips in the wind, and she points her finger at me. "The person causing this whole fiasco." She appears to be in her mid to late twenties, and the wind makes her short jumpsuit conform to her figure.

Charlie keeps his arms around me and steps behind me. "She isn't trying to hurt anyone."

Yeah, because intent means everything. I've learned the

hard way that it doesn't matter. Action is the only thing people will judge your character by. "I'm losing control and need help." I hope she'll take to honesty, because if not, we're all screwed.

Her lavender eyes meet mine, and she stares at me for a moment before taking a deep breath. "Fine, follow me."

"I can't. We were told to find Ria." At least, someone seems kind of helpful.

She props her hands on her hips and looks me over again. "You're looking at her."

A wave of power crushes through me, and the ground begins to rumble once more. I fall to my knees and scream.

"Pick her up," she says and points to Dax, "and follow me. Now."

"Hey..." Charlie's arms tighten, but then he slackens. "She's right. Just get her. You can carry her better than me. Let's go."

Strong hands pick me up, and I'm clutched to a hard, muscular chest. His musky scent reassures me, and soon he's running even though I'm barely jostled.

Wave after wave of power rams through me. I have no clue how long we've been moving, but a door opens, and we're walking through it and into a dark, warm place.

"Shut the door fast," Ria shouts, and she races over to what seems to be cushions on the floor. "Lay her here so she can rest. She should start feeling better soon."

The ground stops shaking, and the Water Artifact stops tugging on me from the outside. "Oh, my God. What is this place?" I can breathe comfortably for the first time since we arrived on land.

Charlie comes back into the room and sits down beside me. He kisses my lips and runs his fingers across my cheek. "Are you feeling better?"

"Yes, the Water Artifact isn't attacking me anymore, and the magic inside me is calming down." I lay my forehead against his and sigh. "I was scared for a minute, but I'm better now. I just want to know why I'm not affected here."

"I have protection spells here." Ria crosses her arms and frowns. "How did you know about the Water Artifact, and how the hell is it calling to you?"

"Watch it. She'll kick your ass." Dax laughs and leans against the wall. "Don't let that little show make you think she's not strong."

Of course, he would speak to my fighting abilities. "I'm here to take the artifact. I have the other three artifacts, and I've come to get the last one."

"That's impossible. I'm the only one who is capable of getting close to it." She lifts her chin up in the air and pushes out her chest. "You can't take it. It must remain here."

"Did you not just see what happened to her?" Charlie's nose wrinkles. "That's going to continue to happen if she doesn't get it."

"Well, I'm sorry." She puts both of her hands on her hips and frowns. "It's not going to happen. It must remain on our world. It's nonnegotiable. We'll starve otherwise. It's what keeps our world alive."

Oh, great. This is going to be fun. "Well, then we have a huge problem here."

"Why is that?" She rolls her eyes. "You're just another entitled person who thinks you can waltz in here and take it."

"No, since I have the other three elements, the fourth one has to balance me out." I get up and walk over to her, standing so we are eye to eye.

She stumbles back a second before she takes a deep breath and stands tall.

I take another step, getting in her personal space. "If I don't take it and soon, I'll implode. Which won't be a problem for you, but how many of your people will I take with me?"

8

Ria tilts her head to the side and purses her lips. "I'm sorry, but it's worth risking the lives of a few to keep our world safe." She stares into my eyes.

"No, there has to be a way," Charlie says as he steps up next to me, desperation clear in his voice.

I place a hand on his arm and squeeze. She must be older than she looks or had to learn some hard lessons at a young age. "She's being reasonable. She's thinking of her world as a whole the same way I'm having to think about things now in my own life." It's the same lesson I learned in the Angel Realm before I could even get the Angel's Breath Artifact, so it has to be relevant in every leader's life, right?

"Chris, what are you doing?" Dax's forehead creases and the corners of his eyes wrinkle.

"Agreeing with her is probably not the smartest." That's an understatement. "But she's being a good leader. I can't fault her for that. She's defending her world just like I'm trying to save myself and our home." I glance at Charlie, and he raises an eyebrow.

"You know what?" Ria purses her lips and rubs her chin. "Why don't you all stay here for a while?"

Now, she wants to make us feel welcome? "Why would we stay?"

"I mean, obviously you can't find the artifact, or you would have gone straight to it." Ria holds out a hand toward me and smirks. "And no one here will tell you where to find it. So why don't you stay here and live out your remaining days. At least you'll find a little peace inside these walls."

"No, that's not acceptable." Charlie's nostrils flare, and his hands clench.

Dax steps to the other side of me. "Are you expecting us to sit here and watch her implode?"

"Just think about it." She looks right at me, ignoring the other two. "With that much power, I can only imagine all the people who are trying to manipulate you and control you. By staying here and living out the rest of your days, you can live on your own terms."

Wow, that's one thing I had never even considered before. The thought has appeal to it. I mean, why would I want to return to Earth? She's right; between Damien, the witch, and council, everyone wants to sink their teeth into me.

And really, who do I have to return to? I mean, yes, my parents and I have been working on a better relationship, but they will be fine without me. Hell, they are so busy reestablishing their own relationship with each other that they haven't even focused on me all that much. So, even though we are rebuilding, I'm not all that close to them.

"You know what?" Ria takes a few steps to the door and grabs a few bottles off of a nearby table. "I'm going to head back to the market and leave you three here to discuss things. I'll be back in a little while." She walks out, leaving the three of us alone.

"Okay, now is our chance." Dax takes a few steps to the door and stops. He turns and looks at me. "Why aren't you coming?"

"Chris, what's going on?" Charlie's hazel eyes are filled with concern. "You can't possibly be considering her proposal."

It's easy for them to be like this. "Well, why shouldn't I consider it? I mean, let's be real. The person I'm closest to is right here with me." Staying here and living my life in peace wouldn't be so bad. "I wouldn't have to worry about the council or everyone else. I could live for me."

"Good to know I'm chopped liver." Dax grumbles and leans against the wall.

"I care about you too, just not the same way." I swear he's a pain sometimes. "And you could stay or come and go since you jump realms. You just couldn't tell Luke."

He crosses his arms for a moment and bites his bottom lip. "Of course, I'd keep your secret, but I wouldn't be able to go back. He'd know something was up and try to find some way to leverage the truth out of me."

"That's interesting. He keeps saying he's on the good side, but that comment right there sure doesn't sound like it." Reasons why I'm beginning to trust my gut in all ways.

"Don't confuse noble intent and ethics." He pushes off the wall and shakes his head. "They are not the same thing. The end justifies the means with Luke whereas ethics mean you always do the right thing."

He's right. Maybe I'm not so ethical anymore myself. Hell, the angels taught me not to be so ethical. Isn't that kind of an oxymoron? "Well, what about all three of us staying right here? I'm not saying we don't still get the Water Artifact. I mean I want to live."

"Thank God." Charlie wraps his arm around me and tugs me against his side. "I was getting worried there for a minute." He taps me on the nose and grins. "Now that I can get on board with. As long as we still find the Water Artifact and you stay with me, I don't care which realm I'm on as long as I'm with you."

Now there is the man I love. I stand on my tip toes and kiss his lips. Butterflies take flight in my belly.

Dax clears his throat and walks across the room. "This is a bad idea, guys. Earth is home. Can we really leave everyone back there to the fate the mirrors display? That demon is stealing souls. I mean, let's see how it goes after we get the artifact, but we need to play the part like we are considering staying without stealing it."

I don't know if I believe the mirrors. At this point, I almost think it's another way the council is manipulating us, but the last part is a good point. "Yeah, but I'm not going to be able to leave this place without getting overwhelmed, so I'm not sure how we're going to be able to find it."

"We'll figure it out." Charlie places his hands on my shoulders and rubs. "We always do."

For the first time since we got here, I take in our surroundings. There are a handful of stairs from the door up to what I'm assuming is the living space and a large square room where we are. There are cushions in various colors arranged on the ground for sitting. Other than that, there is a solid wooden bookshelf across the room filled with thick leather books. There must be hundreds. Other than that, the room is bare.

"What are these books?" For them to be this old, they must be important. I grab one of them and hold it in my hand. There isn't a title page, but when I flip it open, there is spell after spell for water. "Holy crap. This is a book full of water spells."

Charlie walks over beside me and grabs one himself. "So is this one. This one seems to focus on crop growth."

Huh, that's interesting. "This one concerns health ailments."

He puts his book down and grabs another one. "Hey, check this one out." He holds it out so I can look at it.

"Wait..." Would she really leave us in here with this? "That's the Water Artifact we're looking for."

"I thought it looked strange." He stares at it and squints his eyes. "It's just three small round circles of water that float in the air. That's odd."

Yeah, tell me about it.

"Let me see." Dax walks over to us and looks over my shoulder. "That's what we're looking for?"

It is rather anticlimactic when you see it, but it's more powerful than it looks. "It's water. Everyone always underestimates it."

"That I'm not arguing with." Dax takes the book from Charlie's hand and stares at it. "But at least, we all three now know what it looks like. That should help in the search." He puts the book back and places the other two around it like we never touched this section. "But we need her to think we didn't touch these. We need her to think we are considering abandoning our search."

There's truth to that logic as well. That's one reason why I like him around. He helps put things in perspective. "So, she said to make ourselves at home; and if we're going to be here for a little while, I guess we should explore more than just this room."

"Then, let's get to it." Charlie winks at me and grabs my hand, pulling me toward an opening in the back.

Another short set of stairs takes us to a landing. There's a small kitchen-like area to the left. There is no sink but a large glass container of water. There's a pantry full of green vegetables and fruit and a small square table in the center of the room.

"Well, at least there are four chairs." If we decide to stay, there is a spot for each of us and Ria.

"Yeah, but are there four beds?" Dax raises an eyebrow.

"All we need is three, so let's hope for that." Charlie heads out to the landing again and into the next room.

Oh, dear God. Why is he pushing this right now in front of Dax? I need to smooth it over; at least somewhat. "He's right, Dax. We only need three, especially with how my powers are being. It wouldn't hurt to have him close by."

Dax opens his mouth to speak and closes it again. Instead, he simply shakes his head. "Let's go look and see what we have to work with."

Thankful that he dropped the conversation, I hurry out. I join Charlie and glance into the room. It's not a huge room, and there are cushions on the floor like the ones in the living area but longer. They are assorted colors with a thick blanket laying on top of each. That's the only thing in the room except for a small closet in the corner. "They live simply, don't they?"

"Apparently so." Charlie grabs my hand and pulls me out.

We look at the next three rooms, one of which is a large bathroom that looks just like the ones back home. The other two rooms are identical to the first bedroom except that the second and third bedrooms share a bathroom.

"Wow, I expected a little more for some reason." It's very simple, and there aren't any televisions or radios.

We walk back down into the living room when the front door opens again.

Ria enters, and her lavender eyes scan us over. "So... you three seem like you've been busy."

Is she trying to make us nervous? I'm not falling for it. "Well, you did say to make ourselves at home, right? We just scoped out the house."

She stops in her tracks and blinks. "Oh, you did?"

Hmmm... She seems shocked. Why wouldn't she expect us to take her up on the offer? "Yes, your offer was generous, so we want to get acclimated since we'll be staying here a while."

"Oh, that's great." She forces a smile and clears her throat. "I was worried it would take more coaxing, so this is wonderful news."

Not sure I'm buying that. "Well, you had some valid points that were hard to ignore, and you're right. It's not like I'm going to be able to find the artifact, especially with the way the powers affect me outside your home."

"So, does that mean she'll be stuck in here the rest of her life?" Charlie makes his tone sound light, but there is a dark undertone to it.

"Well, no." She reaches into her bag and pulls out a gold necklace with a flat gold amulet attached that's about the size of a half dollar. "This is actually something for you that will help you get outside these walls."

"How does that work?" Dax steps up next to me and stares at it.

"It has the same qualities as the walls of the home, but it's not as strong since it's small." She hands it to me and clasps my hands. "However, you can go outside for a few hours and live a normal life and explore this world."

This is what we need. A way for me to still seek the Water Artifact. "Thank you."

She arches a teal eyebrow and tilts her head. "This is only yours since you're considering staying. If you change your mind, you must give it back. Do you understand?"

"Of course, I do." Even if Charlie and I do stay, I plan on living a long life. I'm going to find that damn artifact.

"All right. Then, why don't you all go out and explore a little, and I'll get everything set up for your return." She takes a few steps back and smiles.

That sounds like the perfect excuse to begin exploring. "Sounds perfect to me. Are you guys ready?"

"I'm ready to go anywhere with you." Charlie grabs my hand and tugs me toward the door.

"Actually, I'm going to stay back and help Ria." Dax's eyes stay firm on her. "I'll explore with you next time."

That's his way of saying he doesn't trust her and wants to keep eyes on her. I've gotten to know him well enough to understand him. "Well, okay. We won't be gone too long."

"Looks like we'll have some alone time." Charlie smirks, and his shoulders relax a little.

Alone time does sound great, but what I'm most excited about is exploring this new world and finding a hint about where the artifact is.

9

Before walking out of the house, I fasten the necklace in place and ensure the amulet is secure. I don't want to chance feeling like I did just a few hours ago.

"Are you good?" Charlie reaches out and gives it a gentle tug. It doesn't loosen and stays in place.

"It appears so." I'm ready to get out of here. I'm not sure why, but the walls are now closing in on me. "Let's go check out our potential new home." Maybe I'll miss Earth more than I thought.

"Have fun exploring the market." Ria turns her back to Dax and rubs the back of her neck. "I told some of the ladies at the market that you may be heading over there soon to check it out. So go have fun exploring."

If that wasn't a subtle way of telling us what to do, I'm not sure what else could be. "Great, that sounds like fun. I didn't get to see much earlier anyway."

"That is a huge understatement." Charlie holds the door open for me and places his hand on the small of my back. "I doubt you would even know your way back there from here."

In all fairness, that's the truth. "Then, I guess it's a good thing you decided to come with me."

Taking a step outside, I hold my breath, prepared for my senses to be overloaded. But nothing happens. The amulet does its job.

"I couldn't risk this cute face never returning." His eyes search me over, and after a second, his shoulders relax. "I mean, what would I do without you?" He pulls me against his chest and lowers his lips to mine for a kiss. "That last part wasn't a joke."

"You'd be miserable for a few days and then move on." I don't want to get serious now. Let's just keep this light. Ria kind of made it obvious they are going to be watching us.

"Chris..." He raises an eyebrow and frowns.

"Now's not the time, and you know it." We can't let emotions get in our way. "Come on, apparently we have some people waiting to show us the ways of this world."

His forehead creases and eyes flash. "No, this isn't..."

"Look, I love you and never plan to leave your side. Can we talk about this later when we don't have prying eyes on us?" I stand on my tiptoes and press my lips against his.

At first, his body tenses, but after a few seconds of persistence, he gives in and pulls me into him. His fingers dig into my back, and I let out a moan.

"Dammit, this is when I wish we were back at one of our places." He growls and kisses down my neck.

My breathing picks up, and I slip my hand under his shirt feeling his lean, muscular stomach. "Tell me about it."

One of his hands roams down my back while the other hand grabs some of my hair, and he tugs. "As much as I hate to say this, we're kind of out in the open, and anyone could walk by. We probably should get going."

Ugh, he's right. What started out as a distraction somehow made a left-hand turn. "Fine, you're right. They are probably wondering where we are." I chuckle and force myself to take a step away, looking to the left and right. There is a row of what appear to be duplexes lined up on both sides of the road. It almost reminds me of the visits to New York City when I had jobs to work on with my parents. We're standing on the walkway between the two sets. They're made of some kind of muddy plaster. "Whoa, are all the houses like this?" It's kind of interesting.

"Oh, yeah." He glances around at them and reaches out to touch Ria's house behind me. "Yeah, the whole way here, it was like this once the houses started coming into view. I guess you didn't notice since you were about to implode." His jaw twitches at the end.

This whole thing has to be hard on him. I can only imagine what it would be like for me if I were in his shoes. "Is it wet? It looks like mud." I reach out and touch the wall. It's cool, but there doesn't appear to be any excess water. Though, it does feel grainy as if there are minerals in it.

He reaches out and touches the wall too. "Yeah, I was thinking the same thing. However, it's dry, so I don't think that's it."

There's a lot we need to learn about this new world, and there's no time like the present. "We better get going before they send someone looking for us." I grab his hand and pull him down the walkway.

A laugh bubbles out of him, and he tugs me back. "You're going the wrong way." He arches an eyebrow and grins. "Do you really think you should be the one leading?"

That's a fair point. "Hey, let me just have this moment." It bothers me that I miss so much when my powers are taking over. If I want to survive this, I have to be aware even when I'm in pain. At least, I have Charlie and Dax here to help me, but that might not always be the case.

"I'll let you have any moment you need." He kisses my lips and gently brushes his fingers against my cheek. "But you're right. We do need to go. Let's get to the market. But let me lead this time." He wraps his arm around my waist and pulls me in the opposite direction.

It only takes a few moments before we find our way there. The booths are still lined up, and everyone is manning their tables. There seem to be a few customers scattered around the area. Some look like us, and others, not so much. There is one person close to us, and he is thick and dark green and resembles an ogre. A few tables down, there is a woman with long white-blonde hair, who's tall and willowy. Her height makes her stand out, but what makes me notice is her pointy ears.

I turn into Charlie and murmur, "Is that a Fae?" The elders told us that they were extinct, yet here is another one standing before me.

"It sure looks like it." He wraps his arm around me tighter and bites his bottom lip. "I wonder how much they taught us is wrong."

We walk over to the section where the Fae is standing. She flips her hair over her shoulder and looks at the merchant. "Can I take my usual, please?"

"Of course. I have it right here." The merchant reaches under the table and pulls out a big vial of water. "That will be one thousand."

The Fae pulls out some strange looking bills that are colorful and appear to be made of wood. "Here you go." She grabs the vial and walks off back toward the pier.

The merchant pulls out a leather bag and sticks the money inside it. She glances up to find us standing there. "Oh, are you the ones staying with Ria?"

Charlie glances at me from the corner of his eye and shakes his head ever so slightly. "We are and just got here today. We had to get out and visit all the sites."

That's one way of putting it. The market is buzzing even in the booths that don't have any customers. There's this positive energy in the air, and it's nice. "I wasn't feeling well earlier, so I wanted to come back here and check out the market."

"Oh, I think we all knew that." She laughs out loud and reaches out to touch my arm. "We sure hope you're feeling better."

I'm sure they do. If they have any sense of self-preservation that is. "I'm feeling much better, thanks." I glance around her table and notice she has bottles lined up everywhere. "What are all of these for?"

"These, my dear, are spells to help the world survive desperate measures." She glances down at her table and smiles.

"What does that even mean?" Charlie's forehead is creased and the corners of his eyes wrinkled.

"I'm assuming that's how the Fae survived." This is the only thing that makes sense, and what does that mean for all of the other worlds we were taught about?

"She's exactly right." The merchant picks up a small bottle and holds it out to us. "This is water spelled to help one form survive. Have you ever wondered why there are times when some crops are bountiful while other farms struggle? This is the reason why."

That's interesting. But that's how they can look like this.

Their city seems well-off, and they aren't in need of anything

"As fun as this conversation is, I'd like to know if there's somewhere nice Chris and I could spend some time together here." Charlie winks at me and rubs his fingers along my back.

"I know just the place. If you go back the way you came in and continue past Ria's, you'll come to the end of the island, and there is a boat ride that's available. It's small, and only the two of you would be on it, and it takes you on a tour of the most beautiful places here."

If it's anything like we came in from, it's not that beautiful—water farm after water farm.

"That sounds exactly like what we need." He glances at the table one last time and looks at me. "Are you ready to go? I think a boat is calling our name."

I want to argue with him, but what if I don't have a lot of time left. It might be the last opportunity I have to spend time with Charlie. "Sure, let's do this. It sounds like fun." And worst case, we'll get a better sense of this world.

The lady beams and rearranges the bottles of water on her table. "You got yourself a good man there. Go spend some time with him."

Charlie and I leave the buzzing market behind and retrace our steps past Ria's.

It's not long before we come to the end of the walkway. It opens up into a wide beach. The water is similar to what I had seen back on earth when I pictured the artifact. It's a deep emerald, and the waves are crashing against the land.

"Wow, this is gorgeous." Charlie takes me forward. "Let's take off our shoes and walk on the sand."

It would be nice to just put my feet in the ocean even if it's just for a moment. I remove my socks and shoes and then dig my feet into the sand. However, it's not grainy. What looks like white sand is actually soft and cushiony. "This is amazing."

He joins me, and as soon as his feet hit the sand, he takes in a deep breath. "I don't know what this stuff is, but I wish the sand on earth felt like this."

"Yeah, that would be really nice. It's almost as if were walking on clouds." I glance off to the right and see a small pier, not too far away, with the boat tied up to it. "Hey I think that's what she was talking about over there."

He glances off to the right and grins. "Let's go."

Hand in hand, we slowly make our way over to the boat. There's something nice about being with him, and we don't have these moments often. A man ducks under the cover and steps out when we arrive.

He looks us over and then glances at the boat. "Are you guys wanting a ride?"

Charlie steps toward him and places something in his hand. "Are you available now?"

"There's no time like the present." The man opens his arm and motions us to enter the boat. "Please sit in the back, and we'll get this ride going."

As I step into the boat, I discover it is even smaller than it looks from outside. There's just enough room for two people in the back with the driver sitting in the front.

"At least I have an excuse for getting so close to you." Charlie's shoulders shake with laughter as his hands rub down my arms.

"You know you don't have to have an excuse for that." I turn into him and gaze up at his eyes.

The driver sits down and starts the engine. "As soon as you two get situated, we'll be on our way."

We both sit down and get comfortable even though it's a

tight squeeze. Charlie entwines his arm with mine, and I lay my head on his shoulder. The boat takes off, and soon we're flying through the ocean with the wind blowing through my hair.

It's strange – back on Earth you can smell the salt in the ocean water, but not here. The two suns are setting, causing the clouds and sky to reflect various shades of purples, pinks, and blues.

It's breathtaking, and for once, my powers are... This is the first time I feel at peace inside since absorbing the three artifacts. Ever since that first day, there's been some kind of imbalance inside me, and it gets worse. Now I know why; I must have all four artifacts inside me to feel balanced, but today I feel just like my old self.

I close my eyes and enjoy the comfort of Charlie and the sweet breeze around me. This is the most relaxed I've felt sense Beth's death. "I could get used to the idea of living here. It's beautiful and peaceful."

Charlie kisses me on the forehead. "Me too. Either way, we have to figure something out. There's no way I will lose you."

Not sure what else to say, I remain silent. However, at least this amulet is working. I open my eyes and take in the view as we drive past beautiful islands full of flowers in various shades of oranges and yellows and greens. They're small but beautiful islands. Not big enough for anyone to live on.

The tour takes about an hour, but Charlie and I get to spend some alone time together. When we pull back up at the pier, the man gets out and smiles. "Did you enjoy the trip?"

"We sure did." Charlie jumps out of the boat and reaches in to help me out.

We'll need to do this again. "Thank you so much."

The suns are almost all the way down, and one moon is now beginning to rise in the sky. We head back the way we came walking on the cloud-like sand. The water looks even more beautiful with various shades of light blue mixing in with the usual emerald green color.

"What do you say we put our feet in the water?" Charlie gazes at the beautiful waves as they crash down.

That actually sounds like a great idea. Who knows how long it's been since I've done something like that just for fun? "I'll race you." I drop my shoes and socks and run toward the water.

"You know you won't win." Charlie soon catches up. "I told you that you wouldn't be able to beat me."

I laugh loud when he catches up to me at the edge of the water. He grabs me by my waist and twirls me in the air, setting me down in the surf. I gaze into his eyes as he lowers his lips to touch mine.

Something connects to me—power pulses through and up my legs and into my core, tugging at the other three elements inside me. The longer I stay in the water, the stronger the connection gets.

His eyes widen, and he pulls back. "Chris, what's wrong?"

Jerking out of his arms, I stumble out of the water. As soon as I break free, the connection begins to fade. Holy shit. "The water is linked to the artifact. That's why they don't want me to take it. Their land will die since water is what fuels everything here." But I'm not gonna survive if I don't.

10

"**C**ome on, let's get away from the water." Charlie takes my hand and pulls me back.

"Hey, are you upset?" We just had a wonderful evening together, and I hate to end it this way.

He takes in a deep breath and turns to face me. "I thought this would be a great evening, and then I ended up putting you in danger."

Is he crazy? "That's the best time I've had in years. You didn't put my life in danger. If anything, we figured out part of the puzzle."

He runs a hand through his hair and shakes his head. "I came here to protect you."

"And you've done that. I wouldn't have survived the market without you." He's the reason I calmed down and didn't implode like I did back at the mansion.

"Let's head back to Ria's. You've been out here too long." He gives me a small smile and intertwines his fingers with mine.

We begin the trek back that way slowly. The silence is

comfortable, and as we walk past the houses, we notice the lights are on.

"It looks like people are starting to make it back home." There are a few people now passing us on the walkway. They have carts filled with the things they were selling at the market.

"Bet that's the hardest thing. Finding a place to store all the merchandise." Charlie looks at each person.

The closer we get to Ria's, the more crowded the walkway becomes.

All of a sudden, a loud voice fills the air. "I'm sorry, you cracked the flask. There isn't anything I can do."

What the hell is going on? "Someone sounds like they are in trouble."

He nods his head and begin taking steps that way. "Yeah, let's go check it out."

We break into a jog, following the voices, and soon we find a tall ogre-like man hovering over the market lady who was talking to us earlier.

His nostrils are flaring, and his green face even has a red hue to it. He's holding a weird contraption that reminds me of a hot vapor machine back on Earth. There is a bottle-like container on top that holds water. "I just need you to fix this. I can't afford a new one."

The lady's eyes widen, and she throws both hands in the air. "I can't fix the fan inside. I'm sorry. The only thing you can do is buy a new spell."

"Then switch it out." He takes a menacing step toward her. "And do it now. I need to get back to my wife."

What's that spell that he needs so bad? He seems determined to get it, but I'm not sure he's going about it the right way.

"Sir?" Charlie steps forward and glances between the two. "Is there something I can help you with?"

"No." His tone is getting low, and his hands clench. "All I need her to do is to give me a new fan, and I'll be on my way."

"But the fans have a spell on them too. It costs me a lot of money and time to do." She straightens her shoulders and stares him in the eye. "You will have to pay for a brand-new one just like everyone else."

"That's impossible. I don't have the money for another spell. This took our savings." His body becomes tense, and his breathing becomes ragged. "I just need you to do this."

"Absolutely not. If I do this for one person, more will expect the same in return." Her eyes hardened, and she places her hands on her hips. "If you keep this up, you will not be welcome back here."

He growls and takes a step forward and grabs her, lifting her up by her shirt. "I'm sorry if I gave you the impression that there was an option."

Tide emerges from the dark shadows and steps in front of them. "We don't take threats kindly here. Why don't you get your stuff and move along?" He turns toward the merchant. "Are you okay, Melody?"

She shakes her head no and takes a deep breath.

There's something missing here. Some sort of explanation. Neither Tide nor the merchant is acting surprised by this man's actions.

"Why don't our two new visitors go back to their house?" Tide glances at us and motions in the direction of Ria's house.

"Are you both scared for our audience?" The ogre taunts and takes a step toward me. "Maybe if I take something important of yours, you'll finally help me with my request."

If somebody doesn't intervene soon, something bad is going to happen. "I don't think threatening them is the best way to go about it."

His stony eyes turn toward me. "I don't think I remember asking for anyone's opinion. I just need this fixed, and I'll be on my way. I don't want to cause any problems." He turns back to them suddenly and throws her against the wall.

Her head hits with a loud thud, and she cries out in pain. Then, he's holding her up in the air by her shoulders.

Dax appears and stands beside me. He crosses his arms, causing his muscles to bulge. "Looks like I got here just in time."

At this point, more backup is appreciated. I turn my attention back to the ogre. "Why don't you calm down, and we can talk through this."

"That's the thing. There is no talking through this." He focuses back on the lady, and he sneers. "There's only one resolution, and she will provide it to me." He places his hand around her throat, and she begins to squirm.

Is Tide not going to do anything? He appears to be a ruler of this world, yet he's letting one of his own merchants be hurt.

"Just... Let her down." Tide takes a few steps back and away from the ogre.

Nope, this isn't going to happen. Not while I'm here. I take a few steps, but an arm catches me.

"Don't worry. I've got it." Dax grabs the ogre by his shoulder and yanks him back.

The ogre stumbles back and releases her, using both hands to catch the contraption that contains water. He spins around and faces Dax. "What the hell was that for?"

Charlie steps forward, blocking me from the ogre's view. "You don't need to threaten this lady."

What I've now learned is there is always more to the story than what meets the eye. Everyone assumed I did the council wrong, so couldn't this be the same thing?

"You'll pay for this." The merchant straightens and rubs her neck. "There's no chance in hell that I'll ever help you again."

"Don't ever come back on this world." Tide takes a few steps and places his fingers loosely through his belt loops. "You will not be allowed in the portal again."

"You won't help me now so what's the difference." The ogre quivers and takes a step toward both of them.

Dax steps in front of them and holds out a hand. "To get to her, you'll have to go through me."

"Come on. Let's get out of here before something happens." Charlie grabs my arm to pull me toward the house.

No, for some reason, this is where I'm supposed to be. I can feel it in my bones. Magic begins to claw around inside me, the brown Earth Artifact along with the blue Angel's Breath. It's as if they're trying to communicate with me, but I'm still not sure what they're telling me. I jerk my arm out of Charlie's hand and confront the ogre. "What's so important that you're willing to hurt someone over it?" My question must catch him off guard, because his attention snaps right to me.

"Do you think I enjoy this?" The ogre throws his hand not holding the gadget up as if in surrender and then rubs it down his face. "I need this. I have to have this."

"But why?" I come right up to him despite Charlie's grumbles. "I just want to understand. There's more here than meets the eye."

A tear forms in the corner of his eye; he brushes it away. "It's my wife. She needs the spell in order to survive."

"What?" Charlie steps up beside me so close our arms brush.

"What kind of spell is it?" Now this makes more sense to me.

"I'm not sure." But the ogre points at the merchant. "But she sure does. She sold this to me just a few weeks ago and said it should last at least two years."

"And it should have, but he broke the fan." Her voice is stern and her face indifferent.

"All he has to do is buy a new spell." Tide glares at me and points to the vapor machine. "She has plenty." Then he motions toward her cart.

"I think that's the problem." Dax moves so that he's still in between the ogre and the water world people.

"Yes, we had to sell our land in order to afford this." The ogre rubs his eyes, and he shakes his head. "But with it leaking, it only lasted a few weeks. I can't afford another spell; we have nothing left to sell."

So that's what this all comes down to. Not only does the artifact power their own water source, but this is how they make their living. However, the greed in their eyes reminds me of the council back home. Maybe this place isn't so different after all.

My powers, still churning inside me, are telling me something. I glance at the spelled vapor machine. Hmmm... I wonder if I could help them out in some way?

"Chris, what are you thinking?" Concern shines deep within Charlie's eyes, and he reaches for my hand.

I'm not sure what to do or what I'm thinking, but the artifacts are tugging me toward the contraption.

"Do you mind if I hold that for a moment?" I reach out my hands toward it, but force myself to stop. For some reason, an overwhelming urge to grab it from him courses through me. What the hell is going on?

"What do you think you're doing?" He jerks away and cradles it. "I won't have this ruined."

The power rises inside me, and the amulet burns on my chest. I don't understand. Charlie takes a step my direction, and I hold up a hand. Something isn't right with me, and I'm not sure what would happen to him. "Don't. I'm afraid you'll get burned."

"What is she talking about?" Tide scoffs and shakes his head. "Is she going to cause the ground to quake again?"

"She needs to get back inside Ria's." The merchant's tone is loud and full of alarm.

"This is ridiculous." Dax stomps over to the ogre and glares. "Give her the damn machine."

"Hell no." The ogre shakes his head and tightens his grip. "This is all I have left to save my wife." His tone is desperate, and he balls his hands up in a fist.

A vibrant flash inside me now courses through from the Flame and mixes with the other two elements. Now's the time if I'm going to do something about it. Using Dax's intervention as a distraction, I rush forward and grab the bottle out of his hands.

"What—" The ogre turns toward me, fear bright in his wide eyes.

As soon as the machine is in my hands, my white healing power mixes with the three artifacts, and my insides begin to warm. It pulses through my body and into my hands.

The dark emerald water begins to glow from the power leaking out, and the glass begins to warm under my touch. It gets hotter and hotter, almost the same temperature as the Flame that burns inside.

"I don't understand." The ogre heads my direction, but Dax stands in front of him.

Moving in between the ogre and me, Dax faces him. "Let her finish. She's trying to help you."

The wind picks up, and a cooling breeze seems to focus right on me... on my hands. My power continues to pulse into the bottle in my hand. The Water Artifact connects to me somehow; it's a dark shade of emerald and flows through the fan and into the bottle. It infuses the water so it doesn't boil or lose the spell from the fire. After several minutes, the glow begins to fade.

My power recedes, and the amulet stops burning. I don't know what happened, but I hand the bottle back to its owner. The fan then begins to run, and a small mist blows into the air.

A laugh bubbles out of him. "You fixed it." His eyes shine, and he smiles at me. "Thank you."

The merchant and Tide stand still, their surprise apparent on their faces.

Now, this is going to be fun to explain.

11

"How is that possible?" The merchant gasps and narrows her eyes at me.

At this point, I realize that we have spectators. Two people are stopped dead in their tracks; they must have seen the whole thing go down. Shit, maybe doing this out in the open wasn't the best idea.

The man, only a few feet away, steps around his cart and shoots daggers my way. The lady next to him grabs his arm, pulling him back. "Don't get to close to her. She can't be trusted."

Tide takes charge. "You two move along. There isn't anything here to see."

"You need to do something about her." The woman points her finger at me and sneers. "She's going to ruin our island for us. She shouldn't have powers like that." She releases the man and heads back to her cart.

"Is the amulet not working anymore?" Charlie's tone is a whisper, and he touches my shoulder.

The power is still strumming inside me, and the Water

Artifact is now affecting me once more, but it's more subtle with the amulet on. "Yeah, but not for much longer."

The ogre turns to me once again, a huge smile on his face. "You don't know how much this means to me." He pulls me into a huge embrace, and it almost feels as if my ribs are cracking.

"Hey, ease up." Dax smacks him on the back. "You're going to hurt her."

"Oh, sorry." He drops me, and there are a few tears in his eye. "I've got to get going, but thank you again." He spins on his heels and heads toward the entrance of the island.

The two spectators head off, and the sky is now dark. However, it's a shade of deep purple.

"How were you able to not boil that water? You used the other elements to fix the fan. The water should have boiled..." The merchant takes a step back almost as if she's afraid of me.

"I..." How can I even explain this? It will just freak them out more, and they appear to suspect I somehow tapped into their artifact's power. I need them to trust me, at least a little bit. The powers inside and out are beginning to ramp up in strength and claw at my skin.

"Right now, it doesn't matter." Charlie rubs the back of his neck and gets so close to me that our arms brush. "She needs to get back to Ria's and soon. Unless you both want another earthquake to happen."

"Now listen here." Tide lifts his head and clenches his jaw. "Don't threaten us."

"He's not threatening you." Dax's low tone somehow echoes against the buildings. "You saw what she was capable of earlier today. Do you really want to push this now when she's not feeling well?"

Tide lets out his breath and closes his eyes. "Fine, you three head back to Ria's before something bad happens."

"But..." The merchant shakes her head and rubs her hands together.

"It's fine, and he's right." Tide points at Dax, and his eyes focus on me. "We don't want to scare our people more than they already are."

"Come on." Charlie grins at me, but there is worry in his eyes. "Let's get back before you begin feeling worse."

Needing his touch to ground me, I wrap my arm through his. "Your touch helps."

"I'm glad." He winks at me and kisses my forehead.

"All right." Dax catches up as we turn the corner and move away from watchful eyes. "I don't know what happened back there, but you've got them freaked out."

"I didn't mean to, but that poor ogre was just trying to save his wife." They could have rectified the situation another way. "I mean they could have given him another glass container. Why did they have to try to make him buy a whole new spell?"

"Really, why couldn't he just use a container at home?" Charlie rubs his chin and purses his lips.

That's a good question and one I hadn't thought of. Did I just make an ass out of myself? But my powers were pulling me to do it.

"Well, while you both were checking out the city, I had a chance to ask Ria some questions when she was putting away her spells." Dax clears his throat and glances around. "Only the glass containers here can handle the spells. Nothing else, but yes, she could have offered him a cheaper alternative."

Why am I so upset that the people here are pretty much the same as back home?

"Well, look who the cat drug home," a deep, throaty tone that's all too familiar calls out to us. The scent of brimstone fills the air.

A giggle echoes in my ear. "She sure does look like she was drug somewhere."

Charlie's grip tightens on my arm, but I refuse to show any hints of annoyance or anger. I turn around and find Damien and Becca leaning up against the muddy looking wall in between two doors.

Even here, the dark shadows around Damien can be seen. His arms are crossed, and a smug smile is pasted on his face. He's leaning toward Becca, who looks worse for the wear. Her blonde hair is plastered to her, and her clothes are so baggy they are almost falling off. The skin underneath her eyes is now black and saggy. It's as if she aged ten years since I saw her a few days ago.

"What are you doing here?" He sure seems to show up at the most inconvenient times. One day, I'm going to wipe that grin off his face.

"Oh, don't seem so unhappy to see us." Becca tugs up her pants before they fall. "I mean, you've always been so desperate to get to me before."

Not missing a beat, Dax steps in front of me. "It doesn't seem like she feels the same now."

"Come on, Chris." Charlie's tone is cold. "We don't need to waste our time talking to them."

No, I won't run away. That's what I've been trying to do all along, and look where it's gotten me. "I'll be fine another minute." My power is rising, but I'm still in control... for now.

"Listen." Charlie steps up and lifts my chin up so I'm looking straight in his eyes. "You don't have to do this now. We need you strong."

"Don't be so hasty." Damien's deep tone is smooth, but

it's like nails on a chalk board. "I mean, I brought you a gift after all."

"That's bullshit." Charlie clenches his fist and pivots to the demon. "You've come here to manipulate the situation."

Dax glances between the four of us, and his eyes finally rest on me. "Let's just hear him out. We're wasting time right now."

"Well, I just wanted to make sure you all were okay." Damien takes a step toward me, the shadows following him. "You've been gone a while, so I thought I should drop in."

Of course he knew when we left. I hate how he seems to know a lot more than he should. "We're fine, so you can leave now."

A chuckle leaves Dax. "You never told me he was so considerate."

"Hey, stop making fun of him." Becca rushes Dax and swings her hand back, ready to slap him. What bothers me the most is she's now moving like a demon. Her steps are jerky and odd for a human.

He reaches out and grabs her wrist. "Calm down, or I'll make you."

She stumbles back and cradles her hand. "Chris..." Her tone is so whiney it hurts my ear.

For the first time in my life, my gut reaction is not to help her. I turn to Damien and raise an eyebrow. "Is this what you were hoping to accomplish?"

A hand touches my back, and Charlie's voice is in my ear. "I'm right here with you."

"I just want to know where the damn artifact is." Damien's eyes flash red before going back to the ice blue. "My patience is wearing thin."

So is mine. "This one hasn't been easy." What does he

expect? Each artifact to appear right in front of me in each realm? "It's being hidden somehow with spells."

Becca snorts. "This is what she did at the Angel Realm. I had to go looking for her."

Before this is over, I may wind up punching her. Taking a deep breath, I choose to ignore her instead. "The Water Artifact is calling to me like crazy, and I'm not sure where it is quite yet, but I'm working on it."

"It's not like they are thrilled with the prospect of her taking it." Charlie's finger stills, and his breathing has quickened.

"So, you don't ask." Damien growls and makes his way toward me.

"Even when I find it, it's going to be difficult." It's so easy for him and the council to say go get the artifact, and bring it back. But hell, it's never simple. "They are going to fight for it. Their water is their livelihood, and the artifact is linked to it."

"If you think you can do so much better, you can get it." Dax arches an eyebrow and moves to my other side.

I'm now sandwiched between both men. I almost want to laugh, but I force it in.

"Huh, and here I thought you cared about your friend Becca." He caresses her cheek.

Becca almost purrs in response like he's her favorite drug.

"What does this have to do with her?" I hate that she is struggling, but I don't know how me having trouble finding the last artifact shows I don't care.

"Well, I mean her soul is fractured, and it gets worse every second." Damien drops his hand and shakes his head. "I thought you wanted to save her. You're running out of time."

"I think it's time for you to go." Dax growls and pulls out one of his knives.

"I agree." Charlie stands tall and glowers at him. "You've made your point, and anything more will just serve as a distraction."

For once, I'm not consumed with guilt. Yes, I brought Becca back to life, but I never meant for this to happen. I thought she could go on living her life like normal. I didn't expect this. If I could do it all over again, yes, I wouldn't save her. But hindsight is twenty-twenty, and I'd never would wish this fate on anyone. I'm tired of feeling guilty. "It's not going to work."

"What does that mean?" Damien places an arm around Becca, and she leans in to him.

It makes my stomach turn. "That's what you always do." I motion to her, and vomit rises in my throat. "You use her against me all the time."

"Stay back." Dax crouches down in a fight position, and Charlie moves closer to me.

"Oh, Chris." Damien pouts, and his eyes flash with amusement. "I'm not trying to use her against you. I just thought you'd like to help your friend who is splintering away bit by bit. I mean, you did bring her back."

"This ends now." I break away from the guys, and my powers pulse inside me. I get in Damien's face and push my finger into his chest. "Stop using her to make me feel more horrible. I'm done. This," I say pointing between him and her, "will not work anymore. If you want the artifact, get it your own damn self."

"There's my firecracker." Dax's tone is proud.

Damien's mouth drops open. "You're bluffing."

"Chris, please." Becca's bottom lip trembles, and she reaches out for me. "I need you."

I won't deal with this anymore, and my power is getting uncomfortable. I turn my back on them and head to Ria's. "Come on, boys. Let's go."

Dax and Charlie walk beside me as we make our way back to the house.

"You'll regret this," Damien calls out.

12

The power's raging through me, and as soon as we turn the corner, I trip over my feet and fall to my knees. Where did this come from, and why so sudden? Is this the end for me?

"Chris." Charlie reaches for me but isn't fast enough.

However, right before the rest of my body has the chance to hit, large arms lift me up. "Dammit, we've got to get you back." Dax sighs and helps me back to my feet.

"Thanks." I hope that Damien is gone and can't see me like this. It would give him too much pleasure. The artifacts begin clashing with my reaper magic, and the Water Artifact feels as if it's rubbing against my skin, causing horrible friction.

"Why didn't you tell us it was getting this bad?" Dax's tone is harsh, and his aura turns that light grey color.

What the hell is his problem here lately? One minute he's sweet, and the next, he's an ass.

"Back off." Charlie wraps his arm around my waist and scowls. "She's under enough stress as is."

My power digs its claws into me. How did the amulet go from protecting me to not in the matters of minutes? I want to stand on my own two feet, but the pressure is building so much that the whole world begins to spin.

"Some of it she does to herself." Dax huffs and rubs his temples. "What are you trying to prove?"

"It'd be nice if we could just get back to Ria's." I'm about to fall apart here, and he wants to argue. What in the world is wrong with him? "Then, maybe you could lecture me?"

Charlie transfers some of my weight toward him and sets a slow, steady pace.

"I'll just carry her." Dax grabs my arm and pulls me toward him.

Oh, hell no. I won't be manhandled. I let out some of the vibrant purple strand, which burns his hand. "Do not touch me like that again."

"Shit." He yelps and shakes out his hand. "You didn't have to do that. I was trying to help, for God's sake."

"You had a funny way of showing it." The power clobbers me from every direction. Dammit, letting loose some energy wasn't a wise idea.

"I've got her." Charlie wraps my arm around his shoulder, and we move again.

The colors inside me are beautiful. It's almost like a fireworks show on a hot summer night, but the difference is the fireworks are exploding within me. Each burst feels like a sucker punch to the gut, and it hurts to just breathe.

A breeze picks up around me, which pulses and aggravates the power already warring inside me.

"Dammit, Chris." Dax grinds out the words as if he's in pain too. "I can see the house from here. We're almost there."

For some reason, that makes everything inside and out more sporadic. Almost like it knows time is running out.

The Water Artifact calls to me, pulsing and taunting. I still have no clue where it is, but the Elements inside me respond to it.

Something rumbles underneath us, and Charlie pulls more of my weight onto him. "Sweetheart, please try to calm down. The ground is shaking."

My vision becomes hazy, but I press on. I have to get back to Ria's; that's my only goal. "I'm trying."

"This is ridiculous." Dax lifts me up as if I'm a child and begins sprinting to the door.

I want to argue with him, but that would be stupid. Not only is my life at risk right now, theirs are too.

Charlie runs in front and opens the door. "Hurry, she should be fine once she gets in here."

When the door shuts, relief engulfs me. The water element is no longer attacking me, and my inner powers calm down. The colors stop fighting against my dark reaper magic and recede back into my core. Holy shit, that was so close. I'm still cradled in Dax's arms which are tight around me.

"You okay now?" Charlie's hazel eyes shine with concern, and he touches my arm.

"Yeah, I feel so much better." I wiggle, lifting up my head, and face Dax. "You can let me down now. I feel fine."

He arches his dark eyebrow and nods. "All right." He sets me back down on my feet, and I almost stumble. "Easy there." He reaches out to steady me.

"Whoa." The world is standing still once again, and I hold on to the wall just in case. "Thanks for your help."

"That's what I'm here for." He gives me a small smile as the air around him goes back to its usual color.

"Come on, let's get you to bed." Charlie grabs my hand and helps me up the stairs.

At the top, Ria comes into view. She's sitting on the floor cushions with one of the large leather books out in front of her. She glances up and focuses on me. "You're finally back."

"Yeah, we got caught up in the city." I force myself to walk tall and straight. I don't want her to know that I was struggling before we got back. The less she knows the better.

"Dax was getting worried because you had been gone so long." She flips a few pages and stops.

Is that an underlying threat, or am I being paranoid? "Well, he must have caught me just in time."

"You're telling me." Dax's laugh is deep and a little off key.

"So did you guys have a good time?" Ria shuts the book and scans all three of us up and down.

"Yes, we did." Charlie steps forward and kisses my forehead. "I haven't been able to spend time like that with her in a very long time."

"Oh, really?" Her eyes widen, and she tilts her head.

She's fishing now. I wonder what she's up to. "Yeah, between work and the council back home, we are run pretty ragged." Okay, I need to change the subject before she asks more questions. "But we enjoyed our time here. We actually went on a boat ride around the island."

Her shoulders tense, but she takes a deep breath, forcing them to relax. "Oh, really? That's nice. That is one of the more popular attractions here. Did someone tell you about it?"

"Yeah, one of the merchants." Charlie steps next to me and grins. "And boy, they were right. I think we fell in love with your world."

"That's great news." She stands and places the book back on the shelf. "So, have you considered my offer to stay here?"

"You know I'm already on board with the plan." Dax

shakes his head and points at me. "The less I have to worry about her, the better. That amulet makes it a lot easier on me."

If I didn't know any better, I'd think he was telling the truth. Jackass. "Actually, we have."

Charlie rubs the back of his head and bites his bottom lip. "It sure is a hard offer to ignore."

"So, what he's saying is yes, we're considering it." Now that Damien is here and is watching my whereabouts, I'm not even sure if staying here is a possibility anymore. The saying is true; you can't run from your problems.

"The deal is for just the three of you." She arches an eyebrow and crosses her arms. "We have never allowed someone outside our own people to live here, so no additional visitors are welcomed."

What is she getting at? Is she assuming that we would want to bring more people here? "I understand that. The point is to get away."

"Just want to make sure the offer was clear." She glances at each one of us, and her eyes land back on me.

"That would be the point of leaving our old world behind." Charlie squints and taps his foot.

"Well, I just wanted to bring it up again since you had someone show up tonight." She stares at me as if she's watching my every move.

"That someone was definitely not invited by us." Dax steps closer to me; his jaw tense.

Shit, how does she know that? We were all alone at that point.

"Okay, but who was he? Why was he here?" Her lavender eyes glow, and the room fills with light.

What the hell is going on? "Are you following me?" This isn't cool. I refused to be watched here like I am back home.

"No, I'm not following you, but I do have to keep an eye on you." She crosses her arm and her eyes fade out once again.

"That makes no sense." How is that even possible? Is she watching us somehow? "You'd have to be following me then."

"No, that's not true." She motions around us and lifts her hands. "The water told me about the man and the woman he brought with him."

How is she connected to the water? That shouldn't be possible from what I've learned. The more I learn here, the more confusing it is.

"He is not a friend but rather someone who is threatening her." Dax gazes off and purses his lips. "So, it's a good thing I was there so we had more people than them."

"Yeah, that demon is nothing but a freaking nuisance to us." Charlie's tone is low, and he clenches his fist.

"A demon?" Ria stills for a moment, and the corner of her eyes wrinkle.

Having a demon around is never a good thing. "Yes, he wants to know when I'll be getting the last artifact." Might as well tell her the truth. Maybe that will buy me some points with her. "He's been after me to get all the artifacts from the very beginning."

Her breathing picks up, and she takes a step toward me. "You can't take the Water Artifact. We won't allow it."

Does she believe repeating that mantra over and over will make it come true? I got it the first time. "I have no intentions of taking it..."

"Good." Ria cuts me off before I can finish.

What the hell? She didn't even let me finish. "Like I was trying to say; I don't plan on taking it if we can make this work." The damn amulet better not let me combust, or we'll have problems.

Charlie and Dax move in closer each time Ria's temper flares.

"What does that mean?" Ria stomps her foot, and her forehead wrinkles.

"As long as this amulet works and I don't implode, I won't take the artifact." Does she really need me to spell it out? And here I felt like I was dense most of the time. "However, if I begin to implode and think that I'm going to cause havoc on the world all around me, then I can't keep that promise."

"But you have to." Her hands shake, and she points at the amulet. "You took that from me."

"As you said earlier, it's about the millions." For once, I know what's right and wrong. It may have taken me a while to get here, but I'm finally here. "If I realize that I can save millions by making a better decision, then that's what I'm going to do."

Ria glares at Charlie and Dax. "Do something about this right now. You all agreed to my terms."

"Do you think I can tell her what to do?" Dax snorts and raises both hands. "She can control three of the elements. I don't have a chance, so I'm just going to stay aligned with her."

"And I love her." Charlie puts a hand on my back and rubs his thumb over my shirt. "So I will stand and support her."

"But the artifact belongs to us." She marches over to me and gets in my face. "I won't allow you to take it."

She won't allow me? I want to burst out laughing right now. "Well, then it's a good thing I don't plan on asking your permission if it comes to that."

She flinches back as if I slapped her. "You..." She runs her fingers through her hair and pulls. "I don't know who you think you are, but you better watch your back." She shoves past me and marches out the door.

Great, I've made a new frenemy.

13

The next couple of days seem to fly by. It's crazy how well we're acclimating here. After Ria cooled off the other night, she returned and seemed to be in better spirits.

I'm not sure why, but there has been no other mention of the artifact or Earth. She's not home very often, but I'm not sure if it's because of us or if that's her norm.

Dax has even taken to blending in here in a way. He doesn't go very far from me, but he has managed to make a few friends of his own and get little tidbits of information from here and there.

Ugh, I'm not even sure what to wear. I've gotten a few new pieces of clothing from Ria, but it still seems too weird to dress like them. All the women tend to wear longer dresses which is so not my style. I grab an emerald green dress from the closet and slip it on.

"Hey, you about ready?" The door opens, and Charlie walks in. His blond hair is messy, which is the way I love it, and his hazel eyes scan me up and down. "Damn, that color looks great on you. It almost matches the water here."

"It's a freakin' dress." I lift up both sides, letting it fan out. "Why in the world do the women wear these here?"

"Well..." He saunters over to me and wraps his arms around my waist. "I think it's sexy." He leans down and begins kissing my neck.

Warmth spreads through me, and I let out a small moan. "You think so?"

"Damn straight I do." He kisses lower and my breathing begins to pick up. We share a room here, but there isn't enough time in the day, and it doesn't help that I never tire of him.

He throws me down on the cushions and begins exploring even lower, moving some of the fabric. "I love you so much."

"I love you too." I slide in my fingers into his hair and pull. For some reason, he loves that.

A loud knock interrupts us. "Hey, are we going or what?" Dax's tone sounds annoyed.

"Damn him." Charlie doesn't stop kissing me, and his hands begin to creep up my thigh. "Just ignore him."

Oh, how I wish I could. This is just now getting good. I try to push Dax out of my mind, but he pounds on the door once again.

"Chris, don't ignore me." Dax jiggles the door handle and sighs. "You both got me up early to go to the market."

"As much as I hate to agree with him, we did." Is it bad that I still want him to convince me to stay?

His hand stills, and he lifts his head to meet my eyes. "Fine, but you have to promise me something special will happen tonight to make up for it."

"Only if you give me motivation again." Every day, I seem to fall more and more in love with him. I don't even know how that's possible, but we fit together so perfectly.

"Don't worry. I will." He winks at me and gives me one last, lingering kiss on my lips. He stands and pulls me up by my hands. "All right, Dax. We're coming out."

Once I'm on my feet, I readjust my dress to make sure nothing is sticking out, then I open the door to find Dax leaning against the wall with his arms crossed.

"So now you're a creeper?" Was he planning on standing out here the entire time until we came out? If we hadn't stopped, that would be really awkward,

"When you wake me up before the butt crack of dawn, there is no pushing it off until later." He arches an eyebrow and pushes off the wall.

"Dude, not cool." Charlie walks out and laughs. "Now she's going to be paranoid tonight."

Did he just go there? "Charlie, if you keep that up, there won't be anything to get paranoid over." I don't want everyone knowing what we were getting close to doing.

"I..." Dax closes his eyes and shakes his head. "Just let's go. I don't want to continue this conversation."

Nor do I. At least he and I are on the same page right now. "Okay, lets head out to the market." At this rate, I may die of mortification before I even get there. I reach up around my neck to make sure the amulet is there. Thank God. I always fret that it disappeared in the middle of the night or something. I love having it. I feel like a normal person with it on.

We walk out the door and into another perfect day. The weather is comfortable, hovering near seventy degrees, and the suns are out with only a few clouds in sight. You'd think since this is a water world, it would constantly rain, but that's not how it works here. From what we've learned, it doesn't rain here except on very rare conditions.

"I don't understand why you don't sell at the market?"

Dax comes up beside me and purses his lips. "Since you can connect with the water here, you can spell just like the others can, and it would help us appear to be integrating into their society more."

That's a very good question. "I'm not sure if I'm ready for that. We're still getting acclimated."

"We are not in any rush." Charlie takes my hand and squeezes. "We still need to find the Water Artifact. That's where our focus needs to be."

The market comes into view in front of us, and one of the vendors waves at us.

For the past couple of days, we've spent a lot of time here. Most of the vendors aren't happy about us, but there are a few who we've made friends with. We continue our way through the market, and a few of the vendors say, "Hi."

Melody's table is up just a few from where we stand, and her eyes meet mine. "Hey, Chris. Glad to see you again today."

At first, I thought the ogre incident made us enemies, but that next day when she saw us, she came over and apologized for how she reacted. She felt threatened by the ogre, and knew she would get in trouble if she gave him something for free. That's not how things work here in this water world, and she knew Tide was on his way. Ever since then, she's the one we hang out with at the market, and she's even let me recharge some of her items.

Dax walks over to her table and picks up a small bottle of water. "So these are the refills for the vapor gadget that you sell?"

"Yes, and I have a fan that can be purchased. Both parts have to be spelled in order to make the machine work." She reaches out and takes the bottle from him, placing it back on the table. "Please be careful with this. I have to pay three-fourths of the sales price for any item I have here. Even if it breaks, I'm still required to pay that price for using a spell."

That seems really odd. "Why would Ria make you pay for something you didn't sell? You would think that they would make exceptions for accidents."

She shakes her head and sighs. "That's not how it works here. We don't pay by the item we sell; we pay by spell. The charge is for having the privilege of using our water, not selling in the market."

"Well that doesn't make sense." Charlie's forehead creases, and he taps a finger to his lips. "Chris spelled the ogre's gadget the other day, and she didn't have to pay anything."

"Most of us can't communicate with the water like she did." She looks around and then lowers her voice. "Only Ria is able to do that. So we have to ask for her blessing, and then she commands the water to do our bidding."

So that's how they're able to make sure they get a cut of each of the vendors' profits. They're able to control how many spells are done and charge according to what Ria allows. "I hadn't realized that before."

"Yeah, this is how things are done here." She sighs and runs her fingers through her hair. "The truth of the matter is I barely make enough money to get by."

Why would their leaders do that to them? Now that she's made the comment, I take a good look at her. Her dress is patched, and her shoes are a little worn. "Does everyone struggle this way or just a few?"

"Haven't you noticed that only Ria and Tide are well-dressed here?" Dax is looking at the table next to Melody and tilts his head.

I look more closely at the merchants around us. Wow,

those people have shoes that are falling apart and holes in their dresses. "How did I miss that?"

Charlie crosses his arms and taps his foot. "Hey, do you want to go walk around for a minute?"

He wants to go check it out just like I do. "Yeah, that sounds like a good idea."

Charlie and I head off, and meander through the market once more. I'm not looking at the products they sell but the people themselves. It's disturbing now that I'm looking closely. People's clothes are worn out, and many have bags under their eyes. Even the children aren't playing around like they do back on earth. They are staying by their parents, helping them work. There are no laughter and no toys anywhere around. At first, the kids appeared to be well-behaved, but they look just as stressed as the parents.

It does take looking closely to notice how poor they are. These citizens take good care of their clothes, and unless you're really looking, you can't see that they've been patched up. Also, their shoes are hidden by the table, so you don't see them falling apart.

"How did we miss this?" I hate that I believed the mirage they were presenting instead of seeing what was right in front of my eyes.

"It's because they're good at hiding it, and they don't complain." Charlie strolls back toward Melody's table.

"Did you notice anything different?" Dax grabs a few pieces of equipment out of the cart and places them on the table.

That's one good thing about him; he's very observant. Whenever we go anywhere, he's always looking around, taking in the sights. He hasn't stopped since we've arrived here. That's one of the main reasons I'm not surprised he figured it out.

"Oh, thank God." Melody rushes over to me and grabs my arm. "That ogre is back. Tide just alerted me. He's going down there to head him off, but having you here makes me feel better."

I'm sure it does. The ogre likes me since I helped him out. "Did that fan already break again?" Hell, I wouldn't be surprised if it did. It's not like I knew what I was doing.

A loud commotion comes from that direction. Charlie turns and shakes his head. "It looks like we're about to find out, and he brought someone with him."

"This could be bad." Dax sets down the items and heads over to me. "If he threatens her, we're going to take him down fast and hard."

"Damn straight we are." Charlie moves in front of me and stands next to Dax. "No one is going to hurt her with me on watch."

Oh dear God. First they were at each other's throat and now they're bonding over protecting me. What the hell? And like I need protecting.

As the ogre and his wife get closer, Tide is frowning and mashes his lips into a straight line. When he notices me, he shakes his head and glares.

Great, I must have screwed something up royally. If he knew me well, he wouldn't be surprised.

"Why did he let them pass and come here?" Melody's voice shakes, and she rubs her hands together.

When the ogre's eyes land on me, he smiles. "There she is." He points to me and laughs. "She's the one I was telling you about."

Now that they are closer, I can tell that the person with him is a little shorter and has long, green hair that blends in with their skin. Her face lights up.

I glance at Charlie. I don't know what's going on, but this isn't what I was expecting.

The woman with him runs over to me and wraps me in a large hug. "Thank you so much."

What in the world is going on? Her arms crush me, and I struggle to breathe. "Uh... you're welcome." It comes out more like a question than statement.

"Oh, honey, ease up." The ogre comes over and tugs her away from me. "You don't know your own strength now."

Dax relaxes and takes a few steps away. He chuckles and sits on the edge of the table.

Now that I'm not in danger, he's going to watch the whole show and see what happens. I wish I could be on the sidelines like that.

"Can you please keep it down a little?" Tide glances around at the other tables, and his tone becomes stern. "We're making a scene."

"Oh, if you think this is bad... wait." The ogre glares at him and then steps out away from us.

"What's he doing?" Charlie whispers and takes a step closer to me.

"I wish I knew." Whatever is about to happen, I'm thinking it's going to involve me.

"Can I have your attention, please?" The ogre claps his hands and steps out away from everyone so he can be seen. "I have something I want to share."

"You said you wanted to speak with her for a moment," Tide hisses, and his jaw clenches. "What are you doing?"

The ogre ignores him and puffs out his chest. "I want everyone to know that this lady," he says as he points to me, "helped me when she didn't have to. My wife had a severe disease that causes our kind to die in six months. We found out about your world and how you might have a spell that could extend her life. We came here and bought it but shortly after going home, the fan that disbursed the water into the air failed." He walks over to the lady with him and kisses her on the cheek.

Wait. Wasn't his wife sick? This lady has bright eyes and seem energized. Could that be possible?

"After she helped me fix the contraption, I took it back home, and it ran perfectly." He laughs and pulls his wife over with him so everyone can see. "Not only did the new spell help slow her disease, yesterday the doctor said she was cured. He's never seen anything like it before, but my wife is healthy once again."

How in the hell did I do that? My power took control and did it on its own accord.

The market breaks out in cheers, but Ria steps out with a large frown on her face. Her eyes land on me, and she scowls.

Tide walks over to me and whispers in a very low voice. "What have you done?"

Everyone here is happy. The ogre, his wife, and most others are enthusiastic with the news. However, I just pissed off the two people in charge. I'm sure this isn't going to go well for me.

14

As we head back to the house for the day, I can't keep a smile from my face. People were accepting of me. That never happened back on Earth. Maybe this really could be my home.

"A penny for your thoughts." Charlie bumps shoulders with me.

"Oh, just thinking about how maybe we could really stay here." He mentioned he would be okay with it a few days ago, but I don't know if he was humoring me. I couldn't stay here without him.

"As long as I'm with you, I don't care where I am." He winks at me and taps my nose.

"It's just earlier today felt nice." Am I being crazy? "Maybe I finally found where I fit in."

"You know you can fall from favor as fast as being graced with it." Dax lets out a long sigh and rolls his eyes. "Don't be naive."

Shit, he's right. Am I being unreasonable? The thought of making this place home and then something happening where I feel like an outcast doesn't sit well. I don't want to make such a huge change for it to be just like living back home.

"Oh, stop it." Charlie frowns and scowls Dax's direction. "She's happy here. Why are you trying to ruin it?"

"I'm not." Dax lifts both hands up as if in surrender. "I'm just trying to make sure you look at the whole picture. Yes, you saved a woman with a spell you didn't mean to do, but what if you cause a huge earthquake and ruin part of the city. They could just as easily dislike you again."

Dammit, I wish he'd quit talking. I don't even know how I saved that woman. You'd think to do it, I'd have to know the spell, but my powers did it all. They persuaded me to take the machine and fix it.

Oh my God. I'm a reaper. A terrible thought occurs to me. Yes, I have the artifacts inside me, but at the end of the day, my black power merges with the others. What if I didn't heal her? What if my reaper magic killed her and my healing powers brought her back. Just like Becca.

"Hey, what's wrong?" Charlie's eyes fill with concern, and he tugs me close. "Don't let what Dax is saying get to you. He wants to go back to Earth when it's all said and done."

"Oh, stop it." Dax groans and runs a hand down his face. "That's not it. I'm looking out for her."

"Guys, stop it." Just when things felt like they were settling down, now I'm freaking out. "It's just... how did I save her?"

"You have three powerful artifacts inside you as well as the magic you were naturally born with." Charlie takes my hand and squeezes it. "You just knew what to do."

"But what if I didn't?" I can't admit to him my fears right now. Not out here in the public and not until I'm sure. Maybe Dax is making me paranoid now. But what if it's true? "Maybe we should go talk to her. After all, Tide offered them a place to stay here for a little while to relax and make up for any misunderstandings."

"You do realize it's because he wants to monitor them." Dax pulls out the keys to Ria's house and opens the door.

Oh. Why didn't I realize that? I'm becoming too complacent and not paying attention to people's motives. "That's probably true, but it doesn't hurt to talk to her when we know he's preoccupied."

"Let's go inside and relax." Charlie pulls me into the house and kisses my forehead. "We've been at the market all day, and you didn't sleep that great last night. I'll make some dinner."

I want to fight him, but he's just trying to take care of me. "I'm fine. I think a conversation would put me at ease some."

"First off, your stomach was grumbling the entire way here." Charlie raises an eyebrow. "Secondly, you've been pushing yourself to prove yourself to these people. I get you're trying to build a place for us here, but you're going to cause your powers to go haywire if you don't calm down and rest."

How can I say no? "That sounds great. I'm starving."

Dax enters the den with us and flops down on the cushions. "I'm all for Charlie cooking dinner tonight. Maybe we can find a way to make it taste a little less bland here though."

"Well, I'll do my best, but it's hard with fish and algae. They can't really grow anything much more than that here since ninety-five percent of the world is covered in water." Charlie heads to the kitchen.

"You do realize that he coddles you, right?" Dax picks at his fingernail and snorts. "I have no idea why he does. You could destroy this world if you wanted to."

Each day, Dax seems to get a little more opinionated and judgmental. I hate that he just throws out what I could do. Doesn't he realize I'm very uncomfortable with that? "Thanks, Dax. If you keep saying stuff like that, I'm sure people will be wary about me. Can't we just pretend I'm normal?"

"Isn't that what got you into this mess to begin with?" He places both hands behind his head and stares up at the ceiling. "Pretending you were normal."

If he was trying to make me feel as if he slapped me across the face, he succeeded. "You know what? You can kiss my ass."

"Stop being so sensitive." He turns his head toward me and purses his lips. "I'm trying to keep your head in the game. They're lulling you in with fake promises. I need you to focus."

Maybe he's right. Ria and Tide frown at me, and Ria stays away from here as much as possible. Maybe they are pretending just to ensure I don't take the artifact. Maybe they hope I'll combust before it becomes a problem.

"Good. I've got you thinking." He places his arms behind his head and stares at the ceiling. "Remember, this isn't over yet."

"Are you still harping on her?" Charlie walks out and kicks Dax's shoes. "Leave her alone and come eat some food."

———— • ◆ • ————

Lying in bed, I find my mind running wild. I've been tossing and turning the last few hours, but my brain won't shut off. It's so bad that Ria has been home for over an hour, and I'm still staring up at the ceiling.

Charlie's lying next to me, breathing deep and with his arms wrapped around my waist. His breath is warm against my neck, but not even his musky scent brings me comfort.

What if I messed up with that woman? It's taunting me... haunting me. Did I bring her back after death? I hope I'm just worrying over nothing, but what if it's not? Damn those what ifs. Can't they just leave me the hell alone?

There is no way I'm going to be able to rest until I know for sure. Dammit, I have to find out. This is ridiculous. If what I fear is right, then I do need to focus.

Taking a deep breath, I slip out of Charlie's embrace, placing a pillow where I was, and pause.

His breathing remains steady, and he wraps his arm around the pillow.

Should I take offense that cuddling with the pillow doesn't alert him that it's not me? Am I that cushiony now?

I place my feet on the ground, and as slow as possible, I stand. I don't want to make any sudden movements that would cause him to wake.

Within a few minutes, I'm out of the house and standing outside under the purple moon in the empty streets. It's so quiet that a shiver runs through me. It's kind of creepy out here.

The first thing I need to do is locate her. I close my eyes and picture her in my head, and just like the Water Artifact, there are multiple images of her at once. What the hell is going on? However, unlike the artifact, the area around her comes into view. I pull back to get an outside view and finally manage to see something distinguishable. There are waves crashing right in front of the building. It's got to be on the same side of the island where we rented that boat the first day.

It still doesn't make sense why every time I try to locate

something, there are at least twenty of the same images staring back at me. I never had this problem before now. Maybe I should try locating something again on Earth and see if I run into the same issue.

I pull up the image of my apartment back on Earth, and one single image of it appears. Huh, maybe it has something to do with the water around here. There was a video I watched when I was younger that talked about how water can refract an image. I bet that's what's going on here.

All right, it's time to be productive. I've got a house to find somewhere near the ocean side of the island. I get moving and notice that most of the houses are dark. Most of this world must be asleep by this time.

It doesn't take long for me to get to the beach. As soon as I get there, a section of houses comes into view that I hadn't seen. That's got to be it. I need to hurry so I can just let go of this worry. I'm sure it's just paranoia kicking in.

When I get to the side of the building, right before I step out in front of it, a large portal comes into view. It's multicolored and about twice the size as the ones I've seen. I stop dead in my tracks and hide right at the side.

A green arm and leg appear out of it, and all too soon, the ogre and his wife appear.

Oh, shit. My legs are heavy and my heart is beating so fast it may just burst from my chest. "Oh, my word." The lady ogre claps her hand and laughs. "I've always wanted to see Earth before."

"Shhhh, Barbara." The ogre places his finger to his lips, but a wide smile fills his face. "We don't need to wake anyone up."

"Don't be a fuddy duddy." She rolls her eyes, but her tone is quieter. "They are kissing your ass right now because of what went down the other day. I can't believe that I was able to take us to Earth."

"How were you able to?" He glances back at where the portal was. "I mean, you've never been able to do that before."

"I have no clue." Her eyes are wide, and she places a hand on her chest. "I was reading something and saw an image. And my fingers started tingling and something inside me knew what to do." She grabs his arm and smiles. "This is amazing. We can go anywhere."

Shit. What does this mean? Could her soul splinter like Becca's? My worst fear has now been confirmed, and there isn't anything I can do.

How come whenever I try to do something good, the opposite seems to happen? Am I doing more harm than good? Fate must have made a mistake when they gave me these powers.

Barbara throws her arms around her husband and gives him a large kiss on his lips. "I can't believe it. We can now go visit anywhere our hearts desire." She pulls back and places her hands on his chest. "We can even go to that waterfall you've always wanted to see. I can take us there."

Huh, Becca never acted like that. She was always scared or worried about herself, but Barbara is thinking of her husband and where he would like to go. Maybe Becca was some sort of exception since I didn't have the artifacts and had no clue what I was doing. Maybe everything will be okay after all.

My powers begin pulsing inside me, the vibrant purple of the Flame burning bright. It swirls and then flashes as if energizing my mind. I blink, and when I open my eyes, my senses are on overload.

The couple begins to walk toward the house, and I take

one last glance at them before they make it inside. My heart stops in my chest. With the Flame coursing through me, I can see the woman's soul as clear as day. And it's cracked with light spilling through. Oh, shit. Her soul is already cracking.

15

The couple enters the house, leaving me outside and all alone with my thoughts. I can't believe that my worst fears were confirmed.

My power is pulsing inside me now even with the amulet on. Dammit, I better hurry up and get back before this gets out of control, too. The last thing I need to do is have an episode right after what I found out.

I turn around and head back in the direction of Ria's. The power swirls inside me almost as if it knows that it screwed something up. My feet move faster and faster until I'm almost in a jog. The only thing that keeps me steady is the sound of the waves crashing. It seems to calm my nerves even if it's just a little bit.

Now isn't the time to freak out and think irrationally. I'll figure out what my next steps are when I get back in bed.

Turning the corner, I pace myself so I can get back as fast as possible but without hurting myself. My power is clawing me from inside once again. The colors separate from one another, and it's almost as if they are attacking each other. It would be a pretty light show if it weren't so painful.

In what feels like hours but is just a few minutes, the door comes into view. I open the door, trying to be as quiet as possible. I don't want to wake anyone up. My goal is to sneak inside with no one the wiser.

When I enter the den, I almost shriek when Charlie appears right in front of me.

His blond hair is a mess, and his body seems tight. "Where the hell have you been?"

Yeah, we aren't talking about this out here in the open where Ria could overhear. "Let's go to our room. I don't want to talk out here."

"Oh, don't worry." Charlie's tone is rough, and he lifts an eyebrow. "Ria left a few minutes after you."

What? How is that possible? "What do you mean? I heard her come in."

"And we heard you leave." He runs a hand through his hair and sighs. "She got up and tried to follow you, but thankfully, you were already out of sight when she got out the door."

Shit, obviously I'm not meant to be a spy. "I couldn't sleep."

"Why didn't you take me with you?" He tightens his hands, rubbing his fingers together. "I thought we had gotten past this and we were finally a team."

Great, now I've hurt his feelings again. "I'm sorry. It wasn't that. You were sleeping so well, and I wasn't realm jumping. Nothing bad was going to happen. I just wanted to check on the ogre's wife. I was afraid and panicking."

"About what?" He takes a few steps toward me and frowns.

My power is picking up in intensity even though I'm inside and protected. What the hell? It should be calming down. "Well, the ogre said she was healed, so that made me think of Becca."

His forehead wrinkles, and he stares off. "I'm not following."

"Well, being a reaper is part of me just like the artifacts now." So he's making me spell this out. I lower my voice to a whisper. "What if I killed her and brought her back?"

"No..." He inhales sharply, and his mouth drops open. "Please, tell me it isn't true."

Okay, his reaction isn't helping. It's as bad as I feared. "It is. I found her when she was coming back from another realm. Between that and my powers healing her, I had to kill her and bring her back." My heart races, and power begins swirling in sync with it. "Shit, what am I going to do? I can't tell them what happened, but her soul is already splintering." The ground begins to shake underneath me.

"Hey." He walks over and cups my cheeks with his hands. "It's fine. We've got this. It's not like they'll know what happens. And if they figure it out, I won't let them touch you."

Yeah, right. Like he can make those promises. I'm not stupid.

A loud bang echoes against the door. "What the hell, Chris?" Dax's tone is rough from sleep. "Let me in."

Charlie drops his hand and opens the door. "She's freaking out and having an episode."

Shit, and I thought it was just my nerves that caused the shaking. Great, now I'm causing a freaking earthquake in the middle of the night. That is going to draw some attention.

Dax enters the room, and his jaw tics. "You're in the house now?"

"My power is getting more unbalanced." Maybe bringing

her back has something to do with it or just stress. I mean it was only a matter of time anyway, but I figured it would be more gradual. Ha, that's stupid. It's not like anything has made sense, so why would it now?

"We're going to have to find that damn artifact fast." Charlie's hands rub my arms. "There is no way in hell I'm going to chance losing you."

It may be too late. The magic inside me clashes and fights with the artifacts. The colors are separate, but it's as if they are attacking themselves as well. Somehow, it's as if they had been behaving and suddenly decided to act out. The ground shakes in rhythm with each inner pulse. "Well, I'm not sure how much longer I have."

"This isn't going to bode well for us." Dax glances out our window and shakes out his hands. "We have company."

What the hell does he mean? I stumble next to him and find several guards running down the road.

"It's getting stronger here." One shouts and waves the others over. "I think it's coming from over here somehow."

Holy crap. They are able to locate me. How far is this earthquake going?

"We need to get her out of here." Charlie pulls me toward the door, almost causing me to fall on my face.

"What good will that do?" Dax turns toward us and lifts his arms out. "They'll just follow us, and she'll be without the protection that the house holds. It'll just make it worse."

Dammit, I'm screwed in all ways. If I stay, they're going to find me, and if I run, it might get worse. It seems no matter what I do, I'm going to cause problems.

"It's coming from Ria's house." One of the other guards runs over and bangs on the door. "Open up!"

"I'm calling her. We know who's doing it if it's from here." One guard grabs some sort of communication device, lighting the side of his face as he places it to his ear. "Hello, Ria. The earthquake is coming from your house."

Well, the cat is out of the bag now. I'm sure this is going to be a pleasant encounter.

"Yes, we will wait outside to make sure she doesn't leave before you get here." The guard hangs up and turns to the others. "Go around back to make sure they don't skip out the back entrance."

Hell, I didn't know there was a back entrance. "Shit. How long has Ria been gone?"

"She left shortly after you snuck out." Dax leans his head back against the wall and closes his eyes. "I heard the door shut and went to peek to see who left. I figured it was her, but before I could go follow, Ria was walking down the hall-way. That's when I knew it was you who snuck out, but I was stuck here. She paced for a while and then left after a few minutes mumbling about needing to figure out where you went." He rubs his eyes and shakes his head. "Obviously she hadn't found you since you made it back and the guards are looking for the source. She was probably hoping it would lead her somewhere other than her own house."

Of course she did. I'm always one step behind everyone. My heart races, causing my powers to become even more frantic.

"Baby, you need to calm down." Charlie's tone is full of worry, and he pulls me into his arms.

For some reason, it doesn't bring me comfort. Every-thing seems to be pressing against me, and being in his arms makes it worse. It's as if the walls are beginning to close in around me. "I'm sorry, but I can't..." The magic flairs even harder, and the walls begin to shake.

"Dammit, give her space." Dax grabs Charlie's shirt and yanks him back from me. "She's freaking out. She needs air."

That's an understatement. I already have the Air inside me. I need the Water Artifact and soon. "I'm so sorry."

Charlie grimaces and reaches out before stopping. "Don't you dare apologize right now. You've done nothing wrong."

I hate that I've hurt him even though he's being understanding. But I can't think about it right now. I've got to figure out a way to control this storm brewing inside me. My insides are raw, and the claws just keep digging in and hitting me throughout.

"Chris, lock it down. Ria's here." Dax's tone is harsh, but there is a hint of worry in it.

"Don't you think I'm trying?" What does he think I'm doing over here? Having fun? I don't know what's gotten into him, but he's becoming more of a jackass each day. I don't know why the air around him is changing, but the darker it gets, the more he changes.

The front door swings open, and there are footsteps hurrying up the stairs. "Don't move from your places. I don't want her to try to sneak out."

Great, I was hoping I'd be more under control before she got here, but that's not freaking happening. Any chance of making this a permanent home has now probably been thrown out the window.

Ria steps through the door that Dax left open, and her lavender eyes find me. "What the hell is going on?"

If I don't get this under control, it's going to go from worse to worst. An image of a jack in the box springs in my head randomly. Maybe that's the key. I concentrate and push the powers down back inside. They resist but lose some of their momentum. The walls stop shaking, but the ground is still quivering.

"Don't you get it yet?" Charlie's face hardens, and he sneers.

We can't let her know we still need the artifact. I want to interject, but when I try, the magic pushes against me harder. I can't break any of my concentration from it.

"Charlie..." Dax's warning is low.

But Charlie doesn't listen. He lifts his chin in the air and stares her down. "Not only is she at risk without the artifact, we all are. She needs to find it and fast."

"Oh, are we back on that again?" Ria crosses her arms and snarls. "After everything I've done for you all?"

"Like keeping us in your house so you can monitor and control our every move?" Dax arches an eyebrow and stands beside Charlie.

At least they are showing a united front. I wasn't so sure Dax would after he tried to keep Charlie from confronting her just now.

Her mouth drops open, and she huffs. "How dare you?" Her hands quiver, and she balls them into fists. "You all agreed that you would stop seeking the Water Artifact. That's why she got the medallion to protect her."

This is not how this is supposed to go down, but I ruined that tonight. We should have focused more on finding the artifact, but we wanted to give the appearance of settling in. Why did my powers have to go wonky tonight?

"Oh, please. You don't want her to implode in the middle of the square." Dax rolls his eyes. "Don't play the innocent act right now."

And now, Dax is making it worse. Apparently, we are letting it all out now.

"Well, I've never heard such blatant disrespect before." Ria takes a step back and finds me again. "If you're going to push this, there will be consequences."

"I'm not going to stand by and watch her die." Charlie's face turns a light shade of red. "We will find the artifact to save her and keep everyone safe on this island."

"You think we'll be safe?" She laughs hard and takes a step toward the door. "If this is how it's going to be, you leave me with no choice."

Something needs to be done to salvage this. Why can't I get these powers contained? I push harder inside me, trying to smush it all inside my core like a box.

"Well, then I guess you'll have to do what you need to do." Charlie stands beside me and scowls in her direction.

"Then so be it." She turns on her heels and walks out the door.

16

Each step toward the door rings in my ear before Ria slams the door behind her.

I'm not sure what she's planning to do, but I can guarantee it won't be anything good for us. Times like these, I feel powerless even though my magic is ramped up and causing problems. I don't have any control, and I'm not sure how I'm going to make it out of this situation in one piece.

"Well shit, that could have gone better." Dax hits the wall with his fist and runs a hand through his short black hair.

"She's just trying to scare us." Charlie sounds almost desperate, but he holds his head high.

Maybe not if I can't get my shit together. At this point, she knows we are going to go after the artifact. I'd hoped to be a little more discreet, but my stubborn ass had to go investigate tonight, and it's a good thing I did. Earlier today, I was freaking considering spelling some water since I healed the ogre. That dream has set sail.

"Dammit, Chris." Dax walks over and gets in my face, placing both hands on my shoulders. "The ground's shaking hard again. You need to get it together, or you're going to kill us all."

"Hey, back off her." Charlie comes up and pushes him on the chest, making him step away from me. "She's struggling. Give her space."

Their fighting isn't going to help me any. I step back against the wall and force myself to take deep, slow breaths. Dax is right, and I need to figure out how to rein it in. I picture the lake back on Earth near Charlie and Beth's home. It's a unique spot because it's where the stream meets the lake. It's the place she and I used to hang out when we were in school and she was alive. I visualize the water running and the sounds the stream makes. This is where I felt safe and comfortable growing up, so I'm hoping it brings me peace now.

The walls around me stop rattling once again. Yes, it's working. Thank God, but I've got a lot further to go. Once again, I concentrate on the image in my head. One of my favorite things to do there was to lay down on a blanket and let the sun warm my entire body. I so often felt cold from either my reaper magic or being around other reapers that it was nice to feel toasty warm on those days.

Charlie's fingers caress my cheek. "You're doing it baby. It stopped."

What? I did it? I come back to the present and realize the ground underneath me isn't shaking any longer. I don't know how I managed to do it, but I'm thinking that spot had something to do with it. There isn't a battle raging inside me any longer. My breathing is easier, and I sag against the wall. "It's about time."

"Do you know what happened to cause the earthquake?" Dax walks over and plops onto the bed cushions.

Is this story time or something? "Well, it started after I

realized that the ogre's wife had been brought back from the dead with the spell I cast on the fan." My mind flashes back to just an hour ago. "I panicked and lost control."

"So, that energized the artifacts somehow." Dax taps a finger to his lips. "We're going to have to keep you from high-stressed situations."

I don't hold back a hollow laugh. I can't believe him. I'm always in high stress situations.

"Even though I'd love nothing more, I'm not sure if that's feasible." Charlie's hazel eyes are filled with worry. "Everywhere we go, it seems to be constant chaos."

Yeah, he doesn't have to say that again. "Well, for the time being, I figured out a way to calm down and get it under control."

"Okay, the best thing we can do is get some rest." Dax stands and heads to the door. "Let's get up bright and early and try to do damage control. I'm pretty sure Ria won't be coming back tonight."

I want to argue with him, but I'm exhausted. Sleep seems like a great idea right now. I need to recharge and let my body have time to heal.

"We need to make sure all the others are gone." Charlie purses his lips and looks outside.

My eyes follow but find the road in front of the house empty. All of the guards in the front are gone or in hiding.

"Don't worry." Dax opens the door and glances back. "I'll check everything out and sleep downstairs. I'll yell if anything seems funny." He shuts the door behind him.

My legs become weak, and I stumble to the bed before I fall down. "I'm so tired."

Charlie climbs into the bed and holds out his arms to me. "Come on, let's get some rest."

Not wasting another second, I crawl into his arms and rest my head on his chest.

His arms wrap around me, and he kisses my forehead. "Everything is okay right now."

That's easier said than done. Even though it's comforting in his arms, my mind won't turn off. What am I going to do about all of this? How do I fix what I didn't mean to break? The first step is finding the Water Artifact and fixing the realms from all the corruption. But It seems as if each time I take a step forward, I fall back ten steps. After several long minutes, I bite my lip and blow out. "What are we going to do now?"

"Well..." Charlie's tone is low and raspy.

I startle and jump a little.

"What's wrong?" Charlie turns his head, glancing around the room.

"Nothing, you just scared me. I thought you were asleep." I hadn't meant to bother him.

He chuckles and tucks me in closer. "Nope, I think my mind is racing like yours. But we continue our plan."

"Which one?" Our plans have changed so much I'm not sure which one he's talking about.

"That's fair." He lets out a sigh and tightens his arms around me. "I think we still need to figure out how to live here or at least keep up the pretenses we do. We can blame tonight on an anomaly, and that her threat changed our mind."

Do I still want to live here? It would be nice, but I do have to get my hands on the artifact. "Yeah, either way, you're right. We at least need to pretend."

Silence falls between us again, and I enjoy Charlie running his fingers down my side.

"But, even with pretending, I don't want to spell any

more of the water. I can't risk harming anyone else." It kills me to know that I hurt the woman ogre even if it was unintentional.

"Then don't." Charlie's tone is getting quieter, and he yawns. "You don't have to do anything you don't want to. We can contribute in other ways."

Yeah, we can find another way. My eyes become heavy, and my body slumps more into the cushions.

The suns shining into the room wakes me. A heavy leg drapes over my waist, and warm air hits my neck with every breath Charlie takes. It's nice to be cocooned in his arms. He's my protective bubble. I snuggle into him and try to enjoy the moment.

"Hey, stop wiggling." Charlie's raspy voice tickles my ear. "You may be asking for more than you're willing to deliver."

My heart picks up at the thought, and I giggle.

"I miss that noise." He kisses my neck and hugs me tight.

He's being sweet, but that comment makes the previous night's event spring back up in my mind. Wow, I royally screwed up last night. "Yeah, well, that might be the last time you hear it."

His arm tightens and his tone gets low and hard. "Don't say anything like that again. We're going to figure everything out."

He can't know that, but I don't want to fight with him. Things are only going to get worse if I don't get the artifact and fast. Not to mention, what happens if Ria and Tide figure out what I've done.

The door to our room opens, and Dax enters with a large cup in one hand and the other hand at his back.

"Finally, you two are up. We need to determine our next steps."

The smell of strong coffee fills the air. "Damn, that smells good. I need to make me a cup."

"Well, you are in luck." He moves the hand from behind him to reveal the cup of coffee he was hiding. "I thought you might need some this morning."

"Ugh, I can't win against that." Charlie lifts up his arm and pouts.

"You'll be fine." I rise to sit upright on the makeshift bed. I'm surprised that my insides feel better after what happened last night. I'm still a little raw but drastically improved. I take the cup from Dax and sip. The warmth floods me and seems to sooth my insides even more. "Thank you."

"I thought you might need it after last night." Dax leans on the wall and takes a sip from his drink as well. "What's the plan? The quicker we address it the better."

That's true, but I was hoping to live in denial a little longer. "I can't spell with water any longer. I don't want to chance killing and bringing someone back again."

"It's not like you meant to." Charlie sits up and runs a hand through his hair. "That has to count for something."

Yeah, I'm not sure that it does. A chill runs through me, so I take another sip of my drink; the coffee warms me as I enjoy the sweet taste. Hot damn, Dax sure can make a cup the way I like. Cream and sugar to help mellow out the bitterness.

"You can still spell things like you had planned but deal more with the ones for crop growth and things like that." Dax scratches the side of his nose and glances out the window.

Huh, I hadn't thought of that. It would prevent the whole issue and still help me acclimate here. "That's true."

Charlie takes the cup from me and takes a sip. "Good idea. That solves your problem completely." He hands it back to me and winks. "Your coffee is too damn sweet first thing in the morning."

"That's why Dax made it for me, not you." I stick my tongue out at him and laugh. It feels nice to act lighthearted even if it's just for a moment. I'm thankful we have a plan now, and it should calm Ria down.

"As enjoyable as this is, you should probably go to the market. We're already running late, and Ria probably thinks we're hunting for the artifact." Dax purses his lips and shakes his head. "The sooner the better."

The fun has vanished from the room. "You're right. Let me go change and get over there."

"Give me a minute." Charlie stands and grabs a pair of pants and shirt from the closet.

"I'm going to head on out." Hell, I'm still in my clothes from yesterday, and they aren't that dirty. "Dax is right. I need to get there fast."

"Seeing as I didn't sleep any last night, I'm ready to go, too." Dax takes a huge sip of his drink then heads to the door. "Let's get going."

"Fine. I'll meet up with you all in a little while." Charlie kisses my forehead and grabs a towel. "I need a shower to wake me up since I didn't get any coffee."

"Well, if you were cuter, I might have made you a cup," Dax calls out from the kitchen.

"Sometimes I can't tell whether you guys are friends or not." I step into the hall and point at him. "It's like it changes every few minutes."

"We're fine." Charlie chuckles and glances in the direction of the kitchen. "We have one common goal, and that's to keep you safe and alive."

That might be true, but I'm not so sure it's going to work. I am still clueless as to where the artifact is kept. "All right, I think we all want that. See you soon?"

"Of course." Charlie reaches out and squeezes my shoulder. "I'll be there right after my shower."

"Love you." I walk back into the room, slip my shoes on, brush my hair, and check to make sure the amulet is still on me. I need to be somewhat put together. I'm glad we have a plan and it'll still give me an excuse to work with the water to help locate the artifact.

———— • • • ————

Within ten minutes, Dax and I make our way to Melody's table.

She is rearranging her spells and grins when she sees us approach. "Hey, how are you today?" Her eyes cut to me. "The rumor is you were the cause of the earthquake last night."

Great, so it seems as if the whole world was affected by my meltdown. "Yeah, sorry. My power got away from me a little last night."

"Maybe if you used it for some of my spells, you wouldn't have that problem." She places a hand on her hip and arches an eyebrow. "I mean you made a huge impression yesterday, and I could use your help."

Shit, she hits me up first thing. "Well, I don't feel comfortable with spelling any healing spells anymore."

"Why not?" Her eyes widen, and her hands drop to her side. "I mean you saved someone."

Dax clears his throat and glances at me. "Yes, but she

didn't know what she was doing. She's afraid she could take a life as easily as restoring it."

Thank God he's here with me. I'm not sure I could have figured out an answer otherwise. "Right, but I'm willing to help with the other ones if you're willing to have me."

"Girl, that's fine. I'll take you any way I can get you." She smiles and motions to her table. "I bet you can do miracles for crops, too. You can spell all those while I focus on the healing ones."

It's as if a weight has lifted off of my shoulders since she didn't fight me more on this. "Great. I'm glad that we could work that out between us."

"Well, you better get to work then." Dax scans the table and picks up a jug at the end of the table in the crop section. "This one looks like it might take a while."

"You've been at it for an hour nonstop." Melody laughs and stands beside me. "Why don't you take a break? I think we have a good inventory for now."

Wait... it's been an hour? Where the hell is Charlie? He should have been here a while ago. "Yeah, that sounds like a good idea. You going to be okay by yourself?"

"I've been doing this for years alone, so don't worry about it." She tilts her head over in the direction of Dax. "And if something goes crazy, I've got him."

Dax is a few tables down, talking to one of his buddies. They are in deep discussion, and he appears to be enjoying himself for once. If he knew I was going to take a break, he'd go with me, but I don't want to interrupt them. "That sounds like a fair plan. I'm going to go see where Charlie is, and I'll be right back."

"Yeah, go find your man." She pats my arm and puts a piece of hair behind her ear. "Don't rush, enjoy some down time."

"Okay, thanks." I head back in the direction of the house. Charlie must have gotten caught up talking with someone since he hasn't made it down here yet. I take my time as I stroll through the market, keeping an eye out for Charlie.

After I pass almost all of the tables and am coming to the end of the vendor tables, my heart begins thumping hard. He's not anywhere here. That's not like him. Did Ria come and corner him in the house? Shit, I shouldn't have left him there alone.

My feet move faster and faster until I'm practically running back to the house. My power begins pulsing inside me and hitting my still-raw insides. When I see the house in front of me, I run up the stairs and fling open the door.

When I enter the den, my world comes to a stop. The bookcase in the corner has been tipped over, and the books are scattered across the room. The cushions used for a couch are scattered and there is a hole in the wall.

Holy shit, someone must have attacked Charlie. I run up the stairs to our room and come to an abrupt stop. The blanket is halfway on the ground, clothes are thrown everywhere, and Charlie's shoes are still in the room.

My magic begins clawing into me once more, and the ground begins to shake. Something bad has happened to Charlie. Who the hell attacked him, and where did they take him? The walls begin to vibrate harder, and I spin around, taking in the whole room again. It has to be Ria and Tide, but where would they take him? What are they doing to him? Why the hell did I bring him? He should still be back on Earth, safe and sound.

A banging on the door startles me out of my panic.

Maybe that's him! I stumble downstairs, tripping over my own feet. Maybe this is just a bad dream. When I open the door, I come face to face with a man I've never seen before.

His hair is the same red shade of Hell, and his white eyes bore into me. He raises a hand, and his tone is dark, ominous. "Ria has sent me to deliver a message. She has Charlie, and if you promise to leave and never come back, she will deliver him to you at the docks."

17

This can't be happening. I can't believe that Ria captured Charlie. Even after I shut the door in the guard's face, it's like my world has been torn apart. I never should have left him earlier. Dammit, how could I have been so stupid? It's not like they're actually going to risk the artifact if they think there is even a small chance we would take it.

My vision shakes but I'm not sure if it's internal or external forces causing this chaos. I'm not even sure I care at this point. Once again, I've inadvertently hurt someone I care about. The man I love is now being held as a captive. I don't even know if he got hurt in the fight. How could I have been so careless?

The vibrant purple of the Flame collides with the other elements inside me. The blue and brown strands push against one another. My black reaper magic scrapes against my skin as if it's trying to get away from the others. I relish the pain as it digs in deeper to my raw insides. I deserve to feel what he is feeling.

A howling blast against the windows causes them to

shake and rattle. I need to find Charlie and now. I focus inward, but there is no calming the beast within me. Shit, what are the words I'm supposed to recite so the artifacts go back to their original place? There is no way I want the demon or council to get their grimy hands on them.

I crumple to the ground as the pressure increases and my mind gets hazy. There is no turning back. I just hope they let Charlie go when I'm gone.

A dark image appears right before me... or at least that's what I see. I'm not sure if it's there or not because my vision is getting darker by the second. It seems to take form and fire and brimstone fill my nose.

Are you freaking serious? Damien is going to be the last person I see. He has an uncanny ability to show up at the most inopportune times.

His blue eyes take me in, and he lets out a huge sigh. "No, this can't be happening."

What? I figured he was here to gloat, but he seems worried. What the hell does that mean?

Damien bends next to me and takes the phone from my hand. "Hey, I don't know what's going on, but you need to calm down."

He's joking. Does he really think he can tell me that and it'll happen? "I..." The words are hard to get out. It's as if I'm underwater and can't breathe. "Can't..."

"You're going to have to, or you're going to hurt a lot of people." He glances around and then licks his lips. "You're causing a ruckus on all the lands; granted this one is the one being hit the worst."

Why does he care? He wants the artifacts, so this should be a good thing for him. "Charlie..." Tears fall down my cheeks, and my breathing becomes ragged. The window in the room shatters, spewing glass everywhere. "Kidnapped..."

"Shit." He moves closer to me; the shadows move frantically around him but still cling close to him. "That's even more of a reason for you to get yourself together. Let's get you some air." He takes my arm and transports me to the ocean side of the island.

The water crashes, and the wind blows through my hair. The waves are high, and the ground shakes under my feet, causing the waves to be more unpredictable than normal. The salt stings my nose, and somehow my breathing accelerates.

"If you want to save him, you'd better get your act together." He grabs my shoulder and shakes me. "If you implode, you're going to wind up killing all of us, including him. All of the realms are quivering since you control the elements everywhere."

My heart sinks. He's right. If I implode, I'm going to hurt people everywhere, not just here on this realm. I can't let them have this much control on me. I close my eyes and take deep calming breaths.

"Once you get a handle on yourself, we'll come up with a plan." Damien bites his lip and lets me go.

My powers are still thrumming, but as soon as I begin to calm myself, the pressure inside begins to lighten. I lay back and let my body melt into the white sand that covers the beach. It's so soft I relax into it and run my fingers through what feels like feathers. It's the oddest thing, but moving helps redirect some of the energy inside and soothes me.

I don't know what Damien is up to, but at this moment, he's making sense for the first time since I've met him. The quake is now a tremble, and the wind begins to calm.

"There you go." Damien's forehead loses some of the creases, and he takes a few steps back.

"We have to get him back." The suns are high in the sky.

I'm reminded of all of the times Beth and I use to lay out by the river. "I can't believe they just took him like that."

"Well, if they want to play dirty, you have to do the same." Damien grins and waggles his eyebrows.

That's the thing, I've always played by the rules, and it causes me to get into situations like this. Maybe I should take a lesson from the demon after all. "Like what?" My magic has calmed down even more now that I'm outside and forming a plan.

"You've got the power of air, fire, and earth." He motions to me and glances around. "Hell, you almost took out an entire island. You don't think you can take out a fortress?"

Whoa... "What do you mean fortress? You were just in her house."

He looks down his nose at me and shakes his head. "You've been here for a short while, and you haven't even done some digging around on the people in charge?" Oh, how I missed his condescending attitude. "That's not her permanent place. Haven't you realized she isn't there much?"

"Well, yeah but I thought it was because of us." His explanation makes a lot more sense though.

"Nope, it's because her primary residence is there." He points toward the other side of the island, opposite of the market.

I glance over that way and see a larger building standing off in the distance, separated from everything else. "It's not too huge."

"No, but it's heavily guarded." Damien's eyes flash with red lightning. "I'm sure that's where they keep the artifact, too."

"If it's heavily guarded, we need backup." Now that I feel more like myself, I sit and watch the gorgeous waves crash.

"Ria and Tide cannot be trusted. And I may have the power of three elements, but I can't get too wild with it. I'll wind up hurting innocent people and could even lose control."

"That's why your first goal should be getting the Water Artifact." His eyes dart behind me, and his face changes to neutral. "That way you're completely balanced and in control. And it seems like we may have a few more volunteers."

What the hell is he talking about? No one would be willing to help here.

"You better never leave me like that again." Dax's loud voice echoes in my ears.

Shit, I didn't even think about him. "I'm sorry, but you were busy." I turn around, and my heart stops. What the hell is Brad doing here? "Why did you bring him here?" That sorry-ass traitor stole the stone from me and manipulated our friendship for his personal gain.

"Hey, I'm here to help." Brad throws his hands up in surrender.

Huh, I bet he is. "So you can steal something else from me?" He made it clear last month that it's only about his agenda. No one else matters.

"He showed up at the market saying he had some information for us, and then an earthquake started, and winds blew so strong people had to pack up their stuff." Dax shrugs and pulls out one of his knives. "I figured we should check on you. It's better if Brad stays with me so I can watch him."

"I don't have time for his fake stories." I stand and place both hands on my hips. "Ria and Tide took Charlie. We've got to go rescue him."

"What?" Dax takes a few steps toward me. "That mess back there was from Charlie and not you?"

"Don't remind her." Damien hisses and clenches his hands into fists. "We need to focus on getting him and not letting her spiral out of control again."

"Listen here, demon." Dax spits out the last word.

"Wait, that's why I came." Brad steps in between the two guys and locks his chocolate eyes on me. "I came to offer help from the Archetypus."

"What is that?" Is he just making up words to distract me?

"They were the first overseers of the Reapers until the council took over." He stands tall and puffs out his chest.

"You mean the ones that got so corrupt that there was a civil war, and they had to leave with their tails tucked between their legs?" Dax lifts up his knife, now on full alert.

"They aren't anymore." Brad takes a few steps back and almost trips. "They realized they were wrong."

Oh, dear Lord. The last thing I want to deal with is another corrupt council. "Oh, so they think stealing and lying are still acceptable things to do?" Brad got me in serious trouble with the council when he stole the Earth's Stone from me. They thought I had something to do with it. "I'm done listening. You can go to hell."

"Look, I'm sorry, but we were afraid you were going to give it to the council." Brad rubs a hand down his face and sighs.

"You manipulated me." My power begins to spring alive again, and the wind picks up.

"Look, if I could take it all back, I would." His hands tremble, and he closes his eyes. "I messed up, but I was trying to protect you. I promise, going forward, I'll be honest and upfront with you."

Right now he reminds me of my friend back in high school. The remorse is coming off of him in waves.

"Look, you can sort it all out later. Right now, we have more pressing matters on our hands." Dax laughs and crosses his arms.

"We're willing to help get Charlie back as a sign of good faith. We have a team of fifteen men/soldiers/warriors at our disposal." Brad glances at Dax and back at me.

"We could use additional resources." Damien walks up beside me, and the coolness of the shadows brushes my arm. "Why don't you give him another chance?"

Dammit, we do need more people to help with the rescue, and Brad does seem to regret what he did. I don't know right from wrong any longer. It shouldn't be this difficult, but I want to scream or wake up from this horrible nightmare. I'm not sure if I can trust him, but if he can help me save Charlie and get the artifact, then it might be a risk worth taking. "Fine, but Dax and I will be watching you."

"You got that right." Dax nods and puts his knife back in its sheath.

"Okay, great. I'll go back and get them, but there is one condition to us helping you." Brad cringes but holds his head high.

There's always a catch. "What is it?" I'm sure I'm going to regret asking.

"I need your word that once you obtain all of the artifacts, you won't return to the council." His jaw is firm and he takes a few steps toward me. "The council had no problem throwing the Archetypus out of power when they became corrupt, but now, they are the ones who are abusing their powers. The council shouldn't have access to that kind of magic."

"Not all the council is corrupt." Dax's eyes narrow, and his breathing quickens.

Damien laughs out loud as if he's watching a comedy show.

"You have my word." I never intended to go back to them anyway. That's an easy one to keep.

"Chris..." Dax's jaw drops open, and his brows furrow.

"Maybe Luke isn't corrupt, but the other two are." I'm not going to stand down from this. "I'm not going to allow anyone to have access to my power."

A large smile fills Brad's face. "Then you've got a deal."

18

The crashing of the ocean waves is faint, almost inaudible, and there's just a hint of salt water in the air. Now that I'm calmer, it's time to figure out a plan, but I've got no clue where to start. "We can't go back to Ria's house."

Dax doesn't miss a stride and keeps steady on his path. "Right now, we are going to take in our enemy."

"I need to let my men know that we're staying." Brad glances around, and his eyes fall on me. "Where should we meet back up with you?"

That's a good question. I've got no flipping clue, and we need to move and fast. The longer Charlie is with them, the more worried I get. "Just want to meet back up at the beach? It usually is pretty deserted."

"Yeah, that's where all the tourists go, or at least that's the word on the market." Dax nods, but his eyes never stop scoping out our surroundings.

He's a warrior through and through. No wonder Luke chose him to accompany me everywhere. He's a natural and always seems to be a few steps ahead compared to me.

"Okay, we'll meet you there as soon as possible." Brad turns to head back to the front of the island and then pauses. "Are you two going to be okay?"

"We aren't getting too close." Dax turns around and points a finger at me. "You can't be stupid. We need to spy only, so you can't get ahead of the plan."

Shit, he's right, but how can I sit still when I'm this close to Charlie? Still, if I did something that wound up jeopardizing him, I wouldn't be able to live with that. I hate that I'm put in this situation. I would trade spots with him in a minute if given the chance. He doesn't deserve this, and he's only there because of me. "I get it. We have to save him. I won't do anything stupid."

"All right, good." He heads back in the original direction. "Brad, we will meet you all back there in the next thirty minutes."

"Got it." Brad heads in the direction of where his men are waiting.

As much as I hate it, I do need to make sure I keep my emotions in check and my head on straight. The fortress is getting larger with every step we take.

It doesn't take long before Dax holds out a hand and lowers his voice. "This is as close as we can risk." We've stopped at the edge of a strip of houses, and he's peering through some beautiful teal flowers. They remind me of the ocean breeze orchids back home but larger. Its beautiful teal and blue flowers are long and reach the ground. This one is big enough to hide both Dax and me. The floral scent fills my nose and calms the earth power inside me.

But what's going on in front of the fortress makes my heart drop into my stomach. It was weird that we ran into no one on our way here, but now I know why. It's almost as if the entire city is standing in front of the building. It's funny because the house is bigger than the others, but nothing super grand from out here. The only notable thing is a huge balcony on the top floor that seems to be coming off of two other rooms. There are a few chairs and a table that overlook the ocean.

My eyes find Tide, who is on the ground out front, handing out guns.

Holy shit. It looks like we're going to be attacked by a mob. My chest tightens when I recognize some of the people in the crowd. They were people I hung around with in the market. How could they turn on me like this?

"Well, it looks like we'll be fighting a whole realm here." His jaw twitches, and he taps his fingers on his side.

That doesn't seem to be an understatement. "They even have guns." What the hell is going on? They try to appear peaceful, but this shows otherwise. "We better head back before someone sees us."

"Yeah, we're going to have to do a surprise attack with all that." He groans and turns back in the direction of the ocean. "We need to get a good game plan in place."

The last thing I want to do is go up against them, but they have Charlie. There is no other choice. I'll do whatever it takes to save him. I can't lose him.

As soon as we get some distance from the fortress, my breathing begins to level. We should be safe for now since everyone is over there.

Of course, that's when the sound of footsteps comes from behind us.

Dax grabs a knife from his belt and spins around. He rushes toward the person who is just now stepping out from behind a building.

No, it can't be. "Stop. Don't hurt her." I sure hope she's not here to hurt us.

Dax drops his arm right before the knife would have entered her chest.

Melody's eyes are wide, and she trembles in fear. "I'm not... I'm not here to hurt you." She throws her hands up in the air and stumbles as she takes a step behind her.

"Why the hell were you sneaking up on us?" Dax's tone is hard, and his breathing is ragged.

Shit, it seems as if we all scared one another. I don't blame Dax for being angry. He almost killed her, for God's sake.

"I'm sorry." She flattens down her shirt against her belly and licks her lips. "I didn't know whether I should call out or not. You guys seemed to be on a mission." She glances at the ground and takes a deep breath. "What are you doing?"

"We had to scope out the fortress." For some reason, I trust her, so I'm going with my intuition.

"Chris..." Dax hisses at me and steps in between her and me. "We might not be able to trust her."

"No, you can." She takes a few steps toward me, but Dax blocks her again. She bites her lip. "She saved me. I owe her."

"Leave her alone." He's trying to be protective, but damn. The past few weeks, she and I have become friends. "I trust her."

"We can't be too careful." Dax tenses up and glares at her.

"I swear on the artifact itself you can trust me." She stays put and taps her foot.

This is ridiculous. I trust her, and that's all that matters. I step around Dax and frown. "Ria took Charlie. She told me I had to leave the island in order for her to release him."

"No." She closes her eyes, and her small fingers pinch the bridge of her nose. "This isn't good."

"I can't..." Tears fill my eyes, and my heart feels as if it's going to shatter. "I can't lose him."

"You're not going to." Dax places his hand on my arm and squeezes. "We're going to get him back and kick their asses."

"I hope you're right." Her voice is low, almost a whisper, and she glances back toward where all of the people are congregated. "You both have to understand that even though Tide acts like it, he's not the one who runs the show."

Wait... What does that mean? "He's the one who greeted us here and came to your aid that night with the ogre."

"It's because they knew you were there." Melody takes a deep breath and looks at her hands. She's quiet for a moment as if she's trying to decide whether to continue.

"Just come out with it." Dax's tone is so low it almost sounds like a growl. "You've already started."

She frowns at him but nods. "You're right." She focuses back on me. "It's all for appearances' sake. They work together, but Ria, she's the powerful one. To outsiders, they want them to think it's Tide who is in charge so they underestimate what's going on."

Once again, I fell for the illusion. I could have sworn she worked for Tide. "So how powerful is she?"

"Before you, she was the only one who could really connect with the Water Artifact, and she's practiced and harnessed that gift since she was a young child. She is very strong and has protected these lands since she was a teenager." She rubs her chin and purses her lips.

"Well, she may have, but I have the power of three artifacts on my side." I should be able to take her.

"But you care about people and try to do the right thing." She runs her hand through her hair and cringes. "Ria will do whatever it takes to protect this land. She won't hesitate to sacrifice one person if she believes it will protect many more."

That's the exact thing the angels taught me in their realm. Someone who is powerful should keep in mind the greater good for all instead of one individual. I get it now, but Charlie is too important to me to just let him die in vain.

"Well, she's going to have a big surprise." Dax stares off and balls his hands. "We've got to get in there."

He's more worried about the artifact, but I'm more concerned about my love. "He's right." I'm not sure if she was trying to talk me out of going, but there is no backing down. "We have to go. I have to save Charlie. He's the only one who understands, and I'm not sure if I could have survived this long without him."

She begins pacing back and forth, pulling at the ends of her hair. "Okay, fine." She stops and places her hands on her hips. "I'm in. I want to fight with you."

"No, you don't have to do that." I don't want her to get in trouble and have to deal with the fall out. I can always go back home, but this... This is her home.

"You saved me when I didn't deserve it." She snorts and glances down. "Hell, you've been the best friend I've had here. This is the least I can do, and I happen to know the layout inside."

"I'm sold." Dax points at her and nods. "Let's get moving. Brad and his group should be close to our meeting place if not already there." He takes off back in the direction of the beach.

"All right, let's go." Melody beams and heads after him.

Well, shit. I guess it's two against one, and I'm the freaking loser. I don't like this, but hell, what am I supposed to do? She's a grown-ass woman. I don't want to be the cause of anyone else getting harmed, and at the end of the day, we need to save Charlie sooner rather than later. I follow behind them, eager to get this thing done.

It doesn't take long to reach the beach. I'm surprised to find Brad and his little army there already. They are in a circle, and all but Brad are wearing matching clothes and bullet proof vests. They are dressed in all black with a gun on each hip. Each person there has to be between the ages of eighteen and twenty-five. I guess this is how everyone pays their dues and moves up?

Brad is in deep conversation with all of them, and the man on his left bends down and draws something in the sand. Huh, I wonder if you can draw in this sand.

The guy on his other side points at it and moves his hand higher, and Brad nods while rubbing his chin with him thumb.

So that answers my question. They are looking at something. We are now about five feet away from them, and there's a building etched in the sand that is very similar to the fortress we just saw.

"You guys have a plan?" Dax leans over and examines the drawing.

"We're trying, but we have limited information on the set up inside." Brad rubs his mouth so hard it opens half way. "It's kind of hard to form a plan if you don't know what's going on."

"That's where I come in." Melody grins and taps her foot as she takes in the drawing. "Okay, this section to the right," she says, as she motions toward the right side, "is Ria's room. There is a balcony right off her room that connects with Tide's."

That makes sense since there were two chairs and a table sitting out there. They must meet there at times. "I saw that. It overlooks the water."

"Yes." She bites her bottom lip and cringes. "Right across from their rooms are the entrances to the holding area."

"Holding area?" The guy on the left of Brad creases his forehead. "What do they keep there?"

"Here in our world, we don't have prisoners." She rolls her eyes and shakes her head. "Ria thinks that people might be afraid of coming to visit us if we have criminals here. So, we don't have a prison; we have a holding area."

That may be the dumbest thing I've ever heard. People still come to Earth even though we have jails and prisons.

"It doesn't matter what you call it, the intent is all the same." Dax pinches the bridge of his nose and groans. "But that's a good thing. We know where Charlie is inside the building."

"So we are going here." The man on his right points to a spot in between the areas where Tide's and Ria's room are.

"Yeah." She points to about the second level of the building. "Here is an entrance only we citizens know about. We have to scan our fingertips in order to get in. If you can take down the scanner, you can sneak in that way."

"How would we take out the scanner?" Brad purses his lips and stares at it as if it's the real thing.

"Guns." Dax scratches his nose and glances out at the ocean. "That's the only option we have."

"Well, I can scan..." Melody rubs her hands together and squints.

"Nope, you're not scanning anything." There is no way in hell I would let her do that. "We're going to hide your involvement. They never need to know you helped us."

"She's right." Brad crosses his arms and stares off into the ocean. "We don't want you to wind up in the holding area. The best advantage we have is that they don't know you're helping us, and they won't be expecting you to attack."

"Where do we go once we enter here?" Brad's comrade on the left draws an X on the building where Melody had indicated the door would be.

"Oh, it's not far at all." She closes her eyes and rubs her temple. "You turn right down the first hallway and take the first set of stairs. Once you get to the top, turn right, and it'll be the first door on the left."

"The biggest challenge we have is that half the town is standing outside armed with guns." I realize that Brad and his crew know nothing about my power. "But I'm going to cause some strong winds and earth tremors in order to disorient them so no harm comes to them."

"That works." Dax glances at the men standing around us. "Let's go. The longer we take, the more time they have to get prepared."

"All right men, let's head out." Brad's tone is full of authority.

We all take off with Dax in front. He knows where we're going, and right now, I don't trust myself to be there. I fall in line at the back and stay close to Melody.

She takes my hand and squeezes it. "He'll be fine. Ria isn't a monster, she's just scared."

I sure hope so. Otherwise, there will be hell to pay.

———— • • • ————

We reach the end of the row of houses, and we all stop to see if anything has changed.

Tide is still with the citizens and breaking them up into teams. "You go search the market, and see if she's hiding there." He turns to the next group. "You go to Ria's, and the last group, you all head over to the beach area and see if anything turns up. Chris likes to go there pretty regularly."

The three groups break off and move toward the various directions, but there are about five armed citizens that hadn't been sent away.

"What about us, sir?" A woman close to my age trembles.

"You will all guard us here." Tide scans the area around him but fortunately doesn't see us. "She and her little body-guard may try to attack."

"Now, let's go." Brad pulls out his gun and glances at his men. "They are scared and not prepared."

"Chris, do your thing." Dax jerks his head my direction and pulls out a knife.

I close my eyes to focus. I don't want to see the citizens' terror. I dig deep into my core and tug on the vibrant blue and brown strands.

The wind picks up, blowing hard, and the ground begins to shake.

"No." The same girl calls out with panic lacing her words. "Not this again. We're going to die."

The fifteen people from Brad's crew run out from the building and head straight to the door Melody told them about.

"You won't be able to get in there." Tide growls as he charges them.

Shit, I need more wind. I yank harder on my magic and divert a large rush of wind in Tide's direction. The wind begins to swirl, forming a tornado, and picks the citizens up into the air.

"Don't let them inside the building," Tide shouts as he appears in front of me right before he twists around again.

A gunshot is fired by one of the water people, and it lodges into the building near the balcony.

"Are they seriously shooting while in a tornado?" Why

would anyone do that? It doesn't seem smart to me. At least no one got hurt, the freaking idiots.

The group of men get to the scanner and whack it with the butt of the gun. It cracks down the center and another guy shoots at the door handle. Within a minute, the door is yanked open, and they file into the building.

I push the wind harder, making sure not to injure them, but they aren't able to fight back.

"Oh, Christina." A voice that is way too familiar coos my name.

My heart pounds in my ears, and a cold chill rocks my body. I turn to find Ria standing on her balcony with Charlie in front of her. She has a gun to his head, and her eyes are right on me.

"I see you, so there is no reason to hide." She pushes Charlie, causing him to stumble.

"Stay here. Don't do anything. I need you to stay safe." I glare at Melody and then take a step out, holding my hands up even though my tornado is still going strong. "Okay, here I am. Just don't hurt him."

Her face has a slight pink hue, and her hand quivers as she holds the gun to his head.

Charlie's eyes are wide, and he mouths the words *I love you*.

Dammit, I can't do this right now. He shouldn't be up there in this situation. It should be me.

"Tell those men to stand down, or I'll kill him." Her tone is stern, but there is panic in her lavender eyes.

No, she won't do it. She may be a pain, but she's not evil. No one can kill someone like that in cold blood. "I don't have a way to contact them. Just release Charlie, and we'll be on our way."

"You need to save yourself, Chris." Charlie jerks, trying to get away, but Ria hits him hard in the face with her gun. His face jerks to the left, and then he sags.

"So, you're saying you can't call them off?" Her voice is high pitched, and she holds Charlie up as he now slumps against her.

This has to be a bluff. There is no way she would do it, and the truth is there isn't a way for me to contact them. "No, I'm sorry."

"Then, so be it." Her eyes glare into mine as she pulls the trigger. The bullet enters Charlie's head, and then he falls to the ground.

19

This has to be a dream. There is no way Charlie is dead. I reach out and pinch myself hard to wake myself up from this nightmare.

It doesn't matter how hard I squeeze I can't seem to feel pain. His body is slumped over, and blood is splattered everywhere. How could this happen? He didn't deserve this.

My vision becomes blurry, but I can't stop staring. Something wet runs down my fingers, but I can't tear my eyes from him. The love of my life has to wake up. This has to be some kind of cruel joke to teach me a lesson. I can't lose him.

"Chris..." Melody's voice sounds far away.

She needs to leave me alone. How am I supposed to go on without him? He's my rock, my constant, the one who never judged me. I... I can't fathom...

Someone grabs my hand and pulls it away. "Stop, you're bleeding."

I glance down at my arm, and blood is dripping onto the ground from where I pinched myself. Why the hell is she bugging me about this when Charlie is up there? Doesn't she realize he needs us? "We've got to help him." I push past her to get to the door the others went through.

"No, Chris." Melody's tone is loud and frantic.

Like hell I'm stopping. Maybe I can heal him? It isn't his time, and I need him. I just have to get to him. I break into a run when I'm grabbed by the waist.

"You aren't going up there." Dax throws me over his shoulder and marches me back over to where I was standing

Oh, hell no. This is the wrong direction. I kick his stomach and claw at his back, trying to get away. He's manhandling me, and I don't like it. "I know you don't like him, but I've got to save him." The purple strand of the Flame flairs and pulses through me.

"Shit." Dax flinches, and soon I'm slipping off of his shoulder. He groans and stumbles back a step. "You just burned me."

I glance up at the balcony again, and it's bare. Not even Charlie is there anymore. Where the hell did he go? "I've got to get to Charlie. I can't wait much longer. He needs to be healed." I take off toward the door again, but someone grabs my arm.

"Stop it." Dax tugs me to him and grabs my face with his hands. "He's dead. You can't save him. Don't go in there and sacrifice yourself when there isn't anything you can do."

A bright light glares in my eyes, and I blink a few times. Once it clears, my heart breaks. Shit, Dax is splintering too. There is a large crack now. No wonder his personality is changing. No... everyone I brought back is chipping away.

A sob racks my body, and I fall onto the ground. I can't get any air. My world fades to gray, and Charlie's face haunts my vision. Just this morning, we were cutting up and kissing, and now he's been taken away in the blink of an eye.

What have I done to deserve all of this? I'm doing the

best I can, but it doesn't seem to be enough. It seems every step of the way, I'm losing someone. Why did I have to be the one able to touch these damn artifacts? Why not someone else? Charlie's life was worth more than all of them put together.

At the end of the day, I could bring him back, but what's the point if he's going to be fractured? I can't watch him turn into a stranger, but isn't that better than not having him at all?

Maybe I can find a way to fix him, but hell, even Dax is fractured, and Luke brought him back.

"Chris, please stop." Melody's scream pierces my ear, and something hard crosses my face.

Oh, no. Are they after her? My cheek stings from the contact, and I focus back on my surroundings.

Melody is now next to Dax and her hair is blowing wildly. She bends down and places her hands on my shoulders. "You need to stop."

"How? I lost him." As soon as the words leave, I want to lay on the ground and just cry.

"But you're going to hurt a lot more people if you don't get it together." Her hands quiver despite her firm grasp, and her eyes crinkle. "Look at what's going on." She looks around, emphasizing our surroundings.

The ground is shaking, and the wind is now spiraling out of control and filled with lightning. A section of houses have now been leveled, and another tornado has formed just a few feet away.

Lightning crashes down and then catches another section of houses on fire. It blazes within seconds, syncing with my wrath and pain within. I glance at the balcony where Charlie was killed, and it's on fire, blazing high with revenge.

"You're going to hurt innocent people." Melody shakes her head, and a tear falls from her eyes. "Be better than them."

A bitter laugh escapes me. "Innocent?" I stand and push her hands off of me, and the ground cracks next to me. "They had guns and were going to attack me. They let her kill Charlie."

"But they don't have a choice." Her eyes plead for understanding, and she faces off with me. "Ria gives the illusion of freedom, but it's a lie. If we don't follow her, she makes our life hell so we can't survive."

"So they let mine become that way instead?" Why are they more important than Charlie? He didn't get to survive.

"Chris, this isn't your way." Dax's voice is soft, and his eyes reflect fear.

"Maybe I should change." It feels as if my heart doesn't beat anymore, like it died with him. My hands catch fire, and I close my eyes, relishing the chaos of my magic. I hadn't noticed it until now, but my power is going crazy, and it's pushing through my body. Maybe I'll be with Charlie soon, the pressure is building, and this has to be the end of me.

"Don't you want to get even with Ria?" Melody stumbles a few step backs, trying to stay clear of me. "You can't do it if you implode."

"I'm going to take her house down with me." The tornado begins moving, and lightning strikes every few seconds, torching the ground. That witch is going to pay for what she did.

"No, I mean really get back at her." She glances behind her, and her eyes widen. "The best way to hurt her is take the Water Artifact from her."

"She's right." Dax, for once, seems to be at a loss. He's not reacting to things going on around him either. This might have affected him more than I realized.

It is true that the most important thing to Ria is the artifact. Yes, destroying the city as I go down may leave an impression, but she'll still take it as a win. I can't let that happen. "Okay."

"What does that mean?" She glances from me to Dax.

I lift my hands up and stare at them, wiggling my fingers. It's so strange that they are scorching with red and blue flames, but it doesn't hurt at all. I better get a handle on it because right now I'm a ticking time bomb.

"I have no clue." Dax takes a step closer and stares as the fire dances on my fingertips. "She's kind of scaring me."

Not able to speak any longer now that I'm trying to contain the raging inferno inside me, I close my eyes and focus. Holy shit, I didn't realize how bad it's gotten. I'd been so focused on my grief that the artifacts have taken over inside of me.

My power is swirling so fast inside me the colors seem to blend into one, and I can't separate them from one another. All right, the first thing I need to do is calm down. My ears are ringing from how loud my heart is beating right now. Taking deep, calming breaths, I try to quiet the adrenaline rushing through me. If we're going to make it out alive, I've got to contain this. I can't believe I've put so many people I care about at risk.

Charlie's passing could be all for nothing if I don't get this under control. I can't let that happen; I need to get all of the artifacts and put Ria in her place... for him if nothing else. I imagine a cool blanket in my mind, and cover the chaotic mess inside my core.

"Oh thank heavens." Melody releases a heavy sigh. "She seems to be calming down."

The artifacts flare against the blanket, but I make sure the blanket doesn't slip off and keep it in place over them. I push them down, trying to extinguish the magic further and hoping that this will do the trick. I'm not sure what else I could come up with at such short notice.

After a moment, the ground stops shaking, and the crash of lightning stops echoing throughout the village.

Thank God this is working. I pull the darkness tighter almost as if I'm swaddling the magic inside.

"You're doing it." Dax's tone isn't as tense, and he whistles. "I was worried there for a minute."

I open my eyes and take in my surroundings. The tornado is now gone, but there is a bunch of debris left in its wake. The balcony is no longer on fire, but pieces are falling down as it cools. The ground is streaked from lightning strikes. This once-put-together town now seems as if it's falling apart.

Brad and the other agents are standing off near the building we had originally hid behind. He's frowning and staring at the balcony where Charlie died. It's almost as if he feels my eyes on him because he turns his head in my direction. His shoulders are slumped, and his face is lined in pain. "I'm so sorry."

At least I'm not the only one grieving right now. I can't answer him, but I nod in reply. I'm afraid if I try to speak, I'll break down all over again. I'm not sure I could come back from it a second time.

The middle door of the building swings open, and after a few moments, Ria steps through with Tide following behind carrying Charlie.

My heart breaks all over again. Charlie's head is drooping, and it bobs with every step Tide takes. His whole body is limp, and there is no sign of life whatsoever. I'm about to pinch myself again, but when I reach for my arm, it's sticky with blood.

With each step, Ria stares into my eyes, making sure they never waver. "Just know, we used some of the healing waters and restored his body to what it was. This is a sign of good faith."

Good faith? Seriously? She shot my boyfriend in the head, and by removing the damage, that shows good faith?

"Oh, how kind." Dax's tone is low and menacing. He takes a step toward them and scowls. "You shot him, but hiding what you've done is so much appreciated."

"You better watch what you say." She lifts her chin and snarls. "That could be you just as easily."

"Can you stop with the threats?" I'm tired of this song and dance. At least now, she's letting her true colors show. "What the hell are you doing here?"

"We're giving you his body so you can do whatever your world does for him to rest." She motions for Tide to hand Charlie over to Dax. He takes Charlie's body and holds him close so he doesn't bobble. I'm glad he's taking care of Charlie.

Ria continues her little tirade. "But you need to leave with all your little cronies and soon. I will not tolerate you destroying our world." She turns her head and arches an eyebrow at Melody. "And you, I'll deal with you later."

Melody startles and takes a few steps away from Ria, getting closer to me.

Shit, they're going to punish her. How can they be so cruel, especially to one of their own? I'm so tired of all of these power-hungry, self-absorbed assholes. It ends now. "If you think I'm leaving without the Water Artifact, then you're insane." This jerk is going to get what she deserves, I'll make sure of it.

Her eyes widen, and she pushes her finger into my chest. "You little..."

I lift both hands up and ask for the flames to light my hands once more. It obliges now that I've removed the blanket from over them. Ria stumbles back when they blaze.

"For a short time, I began to care for your world just like I did my own, but you ruined any piece of that now." I step toward her, and her mouth drops open. Good, she's afraid. "Getting the Water Artifact is the only way I can save my planet, so I don't give a damn about yours anymore. Not after you killed him."

20

"Come on, Chris." Brad's hand touches my shoulder, and he squeezes. "Let's go. We don't have to stand here and take this. We need to take care of Charlie."

He's right, and let's be real. I need to get Charlie's body some place safe, especially if I decide to chance bringing him back. It's hard not tearing Ria and Tide apart, though, especially when they are standing right in front of me.

"Fine." I take in a deep breath and hold it for a moment. I want to make her worry while I'm gone. "But this isn't over. I'll be back, and you'd better be ready to fight me."

"You need to leave and now." Ria's lavender eyes glow, and she squares her shoulders. "You will regret it if you don't."

"Don't let her goad you." Dax stands on the other side of Brad where the three of us are united in front of her. "She's not worth it. Let's take care of Charlie."

Shit, that's not fair. They are using my one weakness against me. "Fine, Melody, you coming with us?"

"What? Really?" Melody's mouth drops open, and she blinks.

"Of course. You're more than welcome to join us." Please come with us. I don't want Ria to punish you for helping us.

A small smile fills her face, and she glances down. "Thank you, but I can't. This is my home."

Ugh, I was afraid of that, but at the end of the day, it's her decision. I can't take that freedom away from her like it was done to me so many times. "Okay. Then, I guess we'll see you around." Unable to say another goodbye to someone I trust, I spin around and march back to the beach area where we had gathered earlier. I need to get back to Earth so Charlie's body is protected. I don't trust them here, and they could use him against me again.

Dax and Brad fall in line beside me. It's surprising because even with Dax carrying Charlie, he seems to keep up with no problem.

My hand aches to reach out to Charlie, but I force it to stay by my side. I don't have time for another melt down. I've got an artifact to find, but we need to make a new plan. It's quiet as we make our way between the houses. There isn't a sound of anyone out and about like there normally is. I bet everyone was either playing guard or holed up in their house. I don't blame them; I did mess up their world.

"You know I can just transport everyone here." Dax stops and readjusts Charlie in his arms. Unlike Tide, Dax is being respectful and taking care of Charlie's body.

That's a good point. I was thinking the beach because it's mostly vacant, but hell, what are we trying to hide from? "Okay."

Brad glances at me and then holds out his arms toward Dax. "Here, let me take him while you do your thing."

"Good idea." Dax hands Charlie to him and then closes

his eyes. He doesn't ask for my help, but stays silent for a moment. Then he holds his hand out and circles the air. An opaque portal appears and glimmers in the suns' light. He motions to me. "Ladies first."

Of course, he wants to make sure I go. I step through the portal without hesitation and appear on the other side right in Luke's office at the mansion. In the time that we were gone, his room got put back together. You'd never know that I had a spell here not too long ago.

"Chris?" Luke drops his pen at the table and stands. "Oh thank God. What took you all so long?"

Before I can even open my mouth, Brad steps through with Charlie in his arms.

"What is he..." Luke trails off and takes a shaky step forward. "Is he dead?"

Tears threaten my eyes, and I can't speak. If I have to tell him what happened, I'll have another melt down. Why didn't I think this part of the visit through?

Soon, the room is filled with Brad's comrades, and at last, Dax steps through, sealing the portal.

"Yes, he died not too long ago." Brad's tone is low and filled with sorrow.

Somehow, it breaks my heart further. "I can't listen to this." I step away and grab my head with my hands. I've got to get out of here. "I'm going to go back to my place and check on things. I need to change out of these clothes anyway." I close my eyes and picture my room and leave before anyone can protest.

I transport to my apartment and take a deep breath. It's dark and quiet, and I'm all alone. I haven't had time to myself like this in a long time, and I don't like it. I miss Charlie and see him in every corner. Memories spill through my mind of the times we shared together.

Dammit, I grab another outfit out of the closet and head to my bathroom to turn on the shower. I need time to decompress and make sure they get through the entire story of the water world. I don't want to catch any of that update and re-live his... I can't even think it.

After peeling off my nasty clothes, I jump in and turn the water as hot as I can take it. At least there is comfort in knowing some things won't ever change. I grab some shampoo and breathe in the vanilla fragrance that reminds me so much of Beth. I'm about to lose myself all over again. I don't even have the peace of mind that he's with Beth since she's trapped in some damn room. The ground begins to shake.

"Christina." The dark, condescending tone that I'm all too familiar fills my ears.

What the hell is that demon doing here? I soap up and wash off as quickly as possible. I don't want that jackass to appear in here. I get out of the shower and put my clean jeans and t-shirt on before yanking the door open. "What do you think you're doing?"

"Just be glad I appeared on this side of the door." He smirks. Damien is laying on my couch, his shoes on the leather.

He is trying to get on my nerves, and it's working. "I don't have time for your sorry-ass games."

"You used to be a lot more reserved." He looks up and taps his finger to his lips. "I think I miss it. It was more fun to control you. Now, I have to deal with a nagging, angry woman."

"Look, I have a lot of important stuff to do. Just do us all a favor and go." This was supposed to be my time to think and try to put myself back together.

"I would, but let's be real. You look like shit." He sits and puts his feet on the ground. "And I'm tired of you trying to ruin my plans."

This isn't going to happen. I don't have to stand here and listen. I head back to the bathroom, grab a brush, and run it through my hair.

"Hey, don't you want to know what my plans are?" His voice grows louder with a trace of frustration. "You aren't being any fun here."

Yes, that's what I'm worried about, giving him his desired reaction. I get that he's a demon, but does he have to be such a freaking narcissistic? My power pulses inside me, and a flame erupts in my hand, burning the brush. "Crap." I drop it, and the smell of burnt plastic fills the air.

Damien appears in the doorway and shakes his head. "I'm all for being passionate, but this is way too much." He picks up the brush and turns on the faucet, running it under water. "This is what I meant about you messing up my plans. Every time you have your little 'melt downs'," he says while fingering air quotes, "it's felt on all the freaking realms." He throws the brush, and it lands in the small trash can beside the shower. "This isn't going to work for me. In order to reign over all the realms, they have to be intact."

He's more delusional than I thought. "That is never going to happen." Does he think I'm going to hand the artifacts over to him? Even if I could, I wouldn't. The air whips around the room even though the air conditioning isn't on.

"Oh, sweet naive Christina." He backs away and heads back into the living room, letting his shadows separate and follow him. "You see, I've had something in my back pocket for so long."

No, I can't handle any more shit today. I'm done. "Damien, just go away. I'm not falling for any of your tricks."

"This isn't a trick." He pulls out a necklace and holds it

up. It contains a square stone, and it's almost as if the stone is swirling. "See, I have Beth's soul right in here. She's trapped, neither going to the light nor dark. Stuck in a room with windows, but all she can see is her reflection."

"You asshole." Even though everyone told me he kept her, for some reason, it's different when he's swinging her right in my face. Once again, I'm just a pawn in a chess match that I hadn't realized I was part of. However, I'm going to win it. I'm going to find the Water Artifact and kick everyone's ass who's ever betrayed me. Without saying a word, I stare straight into his fire-crackled blue eyes and vanish.

———— • • • ————

When I appear back in Luke's office, Luke and Dax are there, and I see Charlie on the cot in the corner of the office.

"Where is everyone?" For some reason, I expected everyone to still be here. This throws me off-kilter.

"I've called the other council members; they will be here soon along with our army." Luke is taking inventory of his weapons again and picking out a few.

A dark, black smoky circle appears, and within seconds, Damien appears. "That wasn't nice." He tsks at me.

"What the hell are you doing here?" Dax grabs a sword and points it at him.

"I think he's here to help Christina get the Water Artifact." Luke tilts his head and narrows his eyes. "Am I right?"

"I guess you could consider us allies for the time being." Damien nods, an evil smile spreading across his face.

"Right now we'll take all the help we can get." Luke reaches out and motions for Dax to lower the sword.

Are they being serious right now? "Where's Brad?" At least he'll be on my side.

"He said he'll be here shortly." Dax's eyes never leave Damien. "I guess they went to get reinforcements as well."

"All the realms felt when Charlie died and you could have taken us out. We need to save our world." Luke turns his back to us and then sits down at his normal seat.

Oh, dear God. "Okay, fine. We all want me to get the artifact." But as soon as I do, we all know Damien is going back to his own side. My focus drifts to Charlie before I yank it away. I can't stand to see him so vulnerable.

"Chris," Luke says, as he searches for something on my face, "why haven't you brought Charlie back?"

It's one thing to tell him, but I'd rather show him. "Dax, can you take us back to the water world for a moment?" I picture where the ogres are staying there and hold my hand out to him.

"Of course." Dax steps closer to me and takes my hand. "Anyone who wants to go better get close."

Both Luke and Damien appear at my side.

Once again, Dax draws a portal, and I'm the first to walk through it without hesitation. Soon the other three follow suit and stand behind me. We are at the back of the house, and the ogre's window is unobscured so we can see the couple sitting down eating food.

"See the light shining through her heart." It's brighter than the last time and almost hurts my eyes.

The ogre is frowning at his wife but remains silent. She's jabbing her finger in his direction, and if I'm reading her lips right, she's very upset with him.

"Yes, why is that?" Luke stares and rubs his chin.

"She's splintering from being brought back from death." At least Luke didn't know anything about it.

"Wait... What does that mean for me?" Dax's voice is low, barely above a whisper.

"It means you're splintering as well." Damien jumps in and winks at him. "In fact, you're splintering more slowly than Becca, but faster than her." He nods to the ogres.

No, that can't be. I turn my attention to Dax, and for the first time, the light shines clearly in my eyes. It is twice as big as the ogre woman's. That's why he's changing so much; he's getting worse each day.

"My God." Luke's eyes widen, and his mouth gapes open. "This can't be."

"This is why I can't bring Beth or Charlie back." My already battered heart feels as if someone has just stomped all over the various pieces. "They can't suffer this same fate."

21

I'll be glad when all of this is over, but I wish I knew how to bring Charlie back without risking his soul.

The lady ogre glances out the window and purses her lips. She stands and focuses in the direction we are hiding.

"Come on, guys, we need to go." I don't want to chance her recognizing me and alert Ria of my presence back in this world. "She's going to spot us."

Dax closes his eyes and draws a portal. "We need to head back and meet up with the elders and Brad anyway."

"Yes, they should be back to the mansion at any moment now." Luke is the first one who steps through the portal, eager to get back for reinforcements.

"There is no way I'm going through your portal again." Damien lifts both hands and takes a step back. "I'll meet you all there."

Of course, he has to be high maintenance. I'm not surprised at all. I step through the opaque portal and find myself back in Luke's office. It's only him and Charlie there, so we got back before anyone missed us.

A black smoldering circle appears at the same time Dax arrives back, and the portal closes behind him. It takes just a moment before Damien is back in his full glory.

My heart is numb when I glance over at Charlie. At this point, I'm not sure I can feel anything else and must be settling into shock.

Damien strides over to where Charlie is, holding the shadows close to him in front of everyone else.

Maybe he doesn't want the others to realize how dark he really is? That should have been my first clue not so long ago, but I can't go back in time and fix my mistakes.

"You don't want to try and bring him back?" Damien's tone is laced with amusement, and he stops once he's beside Charlie, inspecting him as if he was a bug.

"No. I just brought the ogre back a few weeks ago, and she's already fracturing." To subject him to that for my own selfish reasons is not acceptable. He should have a peaceful afterlife if I can't bring him back whole.

"Why don't you step away from him?" Dax's shoulder become rigid, and his eyes turn to slits.

"At least he died before you appeared." Luke's hand runs down his face. "You weren't able to capture his soul like all the others."

"Tsk, tsk." Damien wags his finger in front of his face, and his eyes light up with amusement he can't hide. "That's no way to talk to your ally right now. I mean after all, we want the same thing."

I don't want to deal with this conversation right now. I turn the topic back to the ogre woman. "Yes, she's fracturing slower than Becca, but I'm not sure why." Maybe it's because she was around a demon and influenced with negative energy.

"That's interesting." Luke walks back over to Charlie's study and opens up his notebook, flipping pages. "Could it be tied to the elements?"

"How so?" Dax glances off toward the weapons and bites one of his thumbs.

"That's a good point." Damien saunters over close to Luke, looking over his shoulder. "I bet it has something to do with the artifacts."

Huh. "I didn't have any artifacts yet when I brought Becca back, and had three with the ogre." But I'm not sure if it's that the real cause since Damien is involved.

"If that's the case, then if she had all four, maybe she could bring people back without fracturing them." Luke glances out the window and taps his finger against the paper.

I could bring Charlie back with no worries. Could it be that easy? My heart picks up its pace. Dare I hope? "If that's the case, it's even more important for us to get the Water Artifact."

"Don't worry, we'll get it." Dax grabs a gun off the weapons shelf and examines it. "We aren't going to lose you."

I'm thankful that there is still some of the old Dax left inside him. I dread seeing him act like Becca, but that's a worry for another time. Speaking of Becca... "Not only can I bring Charlie back, but Beth too." Could it be so simple to be able to have both my best friend and my boyfriend alive at the same time?

"Whoa, whoa, whoa." Damien raises both hands up, and a cruel smirk crosses his face. "I hate to tell you this, but there is no way Beth can be brought back at this point."

Luke glares at him. "What are you trying to say?"

"I'm not falling for your tricks." Is he trying to get a rise out of me? Doesn't he realize that I'm done with all of his shit?

"Unfortunately, it's not a trick." His tone is condescending, and he lifts his nose up in the air.

What a pompous ass.

"Don't roll your eyes. There's something you might want to know before it's too late for your beloved Charlie." He walks over to Charlie and glances at him. "You see, it's too late for Beth because her body is too decayed. She would look like a zombie if you tried resurrecting her now. There is only a certain shelf life a body has."

Dammit, I hadn't even thought about that. Her body has been decomposing for over two years.

"And you wait until now to share that information with her?" Dax places the gun back on the table and then grab some bullets on the side. Pulling out the gun he always carries, he begins re-loading it.

"So why did you keep her soul if it's too late for me to bring her back?" Why lock her up in that amulet if he knew it was too late?

"Because he still can use her as a bargaining tool." Luke barks out a nasty, deep laugh. "You truly are an awful demon."

"Ahhh, and the elder finally caught on." Damien chuckles and touches Charlie's arm.

Right now, I want to slug him. He's a special kind of asshole.

"I'm assuming our loyal..." he says as he looks up as if trying to search for the right word, "seeker wants a chance for Beth's soul to have peace after all." He arches an eyebrow and winks at me. "Am I right?"

"If I could kill you right now, I would." I'm so over his shit and manipulation. If I had a guess, he orchestrated the whole thing just to make sure I ended up in the spot I'm in now.

"I'm willing to give her to you." He wraps his hand around the amulet and purses his lips. "For a price, that is."

"It's always for something isn't it?" But can I really leave my friend trapped for all her eternity in that windowless room the angels showed me?

"Don't listen to him." Luke slams the book shut and stand. "Demons are sneaky and usually always one step ahead."

Isn't that the freaking truth. "What do you want?"

"Nu-uh... Now isn't the time for me to tell you all my secrets." He tucks the necklace back under his shirt and shakes his head. "That would be too easy. I'll let you know when it's time, but we better hurry before it's too late for Charlie."

Shit, I hadn't even thought about that, but he's right. The longer it takes, the less my chances are for bringing him back. I don't need his body decomposing.

The door swings open, and soon Brad enters. His eyes land on Charlie, but he tears them away and focuses on me.

"Where is everyone?" Dax crosses his arms and frowns. "I thought you said the former council was going to help us."

"Wait." Luke rubs his hands together and takes slow steps to where he stands right behind me. "What the hell are you talking about?"

Oh, this is going to be fun. "Brad works with the original council. They want to make sure the corrupt council members don't get their hands on the artifact." It'll be interesting to see how he reacts to this.

Luke's expression is unreadable. "Why would we want to have those traitors helping us?"

"Because you might need bigger numbers." Brad puffs

out his chest and scowls. "But they aren't willing to join forces with this council, so I'm going to help you and provide them with updates in case we need the extra help."

"We could need reinforcements." Dax nods and claps Brad on the back. "We wouldn't have been able to attack the fortress if it hadn't been for your team."

"How were you able to get to the water world?" Luke's forehead wrinkles, and he bites his lip.

"Don't worry. We have our ways." Brad grins but startles when the door opens once again. Four teenaged boys that appear to be between sixteen and eighteen walk in.

I've never seen these guys before. My power pulses inside me as if it's ready to protect me at a moment's notice.

"Why are you here?" Brad's tone is rough, and his jaw ticks.

"We're your backup." The oldest of the four stands in front and crosses his arms. "They told us to come with you."

"It seems like your leaders aren't very confident in your ability." Damien waggles his eyebrows.

Oh, dear God, I need to diffuse this. "Let's head back and see what's going on so we can make a plan." I need to get moving, or I might go stir crazy.

"That's a good idea, especially since Luke hasn't been there." Dax heads into the center of the group. "Now, everyone touch my arm." He lifts his left arm out as he closes his eyes, drawing the portal back to the water world.

"I'll get there on my own." Damien grins as his body begins to disappear into a dark, black shadow.

"What the..." Brad shakes his head, but we don't have time for that. I push him forward into the portal.

Soon, all eight of us appear on the beach, and the purple moon is high in the sky. I glance toward the town and spy someone standing about one hundred yards from us.

Luke stiffens. "Do we know who that is?"

Oh, thank God. "It's Melody." What is she doing out here like this? Did something happen to her? I rush over to her and scan her for injuries. "Are you okay?"

Melody gives me a small smile. "Yeah, but I've been waiting for you to come back. The town has gotten a little crazy since Charlie's death."

A dark, smoky shadow begins swirling beside me, and Melody's panic causes her to stumble back a few steps.

The stench of hell is somehow stronger here with the waves crashing around us. Damien's blue eyes glow in the dark. "Ahhh, I see you have a little snoop in your mix."

"Why is a demon here with you?" Melody straightens her shoulders and stares straight into his eyes.

"Because I'm here to help her fight along with her traitorous high school friend and one of the council members from Earth who swears he isn't corrupt." Damien chuckles and shrugs. "So, obviously none of us have ulterior motives."

"We are here to help her." Brad glares at Damien as the four other guys flank him.

"When you put it like that, maybe we shouldn't work with you." Dax pulls out his gun, holding it down by his side but ready to shoot if needed.

"Oh, please." Damien rolls his eyes and bumps his shoulder against mine. "We all have a common goal right now – to make sure Chris doesn't implode."

Is he seriously trying to act like we're buddies right now?

"Uh... Chris?" Melody takes a few steps back and grits her teeth. "Can I talk to you for a moment in a private?"

Now isn't the time, but this isn't her norm. "Hey guys, I'll be just a second."

Dax purses his lips but nods. "Okay, we'll begin planning."

"Perfect, thanks." I turn, and we head toward the town but stop when we have about fifty feet between us and them.

"What's up?" Yes, I might be rude cutting to the chase, but I've got to get that artifact and fast. The longer we're here, the less chance we have for a surprise attack.

"Do you really think this is wise?" Her voice is low, and the waves are so loud I can barely catch her words.

Now she's worried about me taking the artifact. "I've got to in order to survive."

She holds up a hand and shakes her head. "No, not that." She points toward the guys we left behind. "Partnering with them. The older guy seems fishy, and there is a freaking demon. I'm afraid you're surrounded by the enemies who are going to take advantage of you."

If I was worried about her loyalty before, I'm not at all right now. "Yes, Damien definitely has ulterior motives, and I think Luke may as well." I already know that Damien's going to try to hold Beth over my head, but I won't allow him access to this power. "But this will be the quickest way to get the Water Artifact, so this is the best way."

"But at what cost?" She reaches out and touches my shoulder, her voice cracking. "I don't want anything to happen to you."

"Don't worry. I won't be controlled, no matter what they try to hold over my head." It's time for me to put the needs of many before my own. My power controls all of the realms, not just Earth. "For whatever reason, becoming the seeker was thrust upon me, and I won't be a pawn in anyone's game. I will not destroy any one's world, and I will make my own decisions without any influence from them. It's time I take control of my actions and stand up for my responsibilities. So, yes, the price will be high, but the realms will be safe."

"Okay, I will support you." She nods and squares her shoulders. "We're in this together." Then, she turns on her heels and walks away toward the city.

22

If she is going to stand by me, why the hell is she walking away from us? I'm at a loss as Melody disappears between two buildings. She never glances back once. What does that even mean?

"Did you upset her?" Luke steps away from the other men and winces.

"No, I don't think so." She didn't seem upset, and she told me she would back me. Would she say that if she didn't mean it? Melody takes her stand on things just like the first night I met her. She wasn't the nicest, but she was afraid.

"That's nothing to worry about." Dax motions for me to join them and smirks. "Melody marches to her own drum."

That's true, but I wish she would have stayed. I don't want her to get into any more trouble than she's already in. There has to be some way I can help her.

"So, we came up with a plan." Brad's face has an eerie look to it as the purple reflects off of his skin. It's as if the moon is pouring all of its glow onto him.

Or at least it seems that way to me, but maybe it's because he's the one delivering the plan. "Okay, let's have it."

"Since we have a surprise attack, we're going to use the darkness to our advantage." He steps toward me and lowers his voice almost as if he thinks someone will overhear. "Then..." A large wave gains momentum behind him, and it barrels toward us. The wave has to be at least ten feet tall.

Shit, there is no way we can get away fast enough. I push past him so I'm closer to the water than everyone else and throw my hands out to the side. My power flares to life inside me, and I ask the wind for help holding off the wave.

"What the..." Luke's eyes widen, and his mouth partially gapes open. "We need to move." He stumbles back, and the rest follow suit.

Yeah, something big is happening. I've never seen waves like this here before. Maybe there is something wonky going on. The wind swirls around me and pushes out the tether that's tied to me. The wind changes direction and instead of blowing toward us, it presses against the waves.

"How is that possible?" One of the younger guys from Brad's group stops moving and watches, motionless, as the wave stands stationary and then begins to drop in size. "Is she doing that?"

Wow, he's a smart one. "Yeah, I am, and you need to back up." I'm still not in full control over these powers, and I don't want to hurt anyone. When the ocean returns to its normal cadence, I lower my hands to my side and try to calm the storm growing within.

The artifacts are beginning to fight and separate from one another once more. Oh, no. This is how I begin imploding.

"You're freaking amazing." The boy hasn't moved, and his eyes are full of adoration.

Why hasn't he moved back? There's a reason I told him

to get away. What is it with men? Just because I don't have balls doesn't mean I shouldn't be listened to.

All of a sudden, it feels as if sandpaper is being rubbed against my skin. I glance at my arms, and there's a coat of thin water appearing all over me, but it's not making my clothes wet. The power of the Water Artifact causes friction as it assaults me.

Of course, the elements inside me respond and begin clawing me from the inside to get out. All four artifacts want to meet and become one. The ground shakes, and lightning strikes right beside me.

"Josh, get away from her." Brad's tone is frantic, and I can hear footsteps as the others rush to gain distance between me and them.

Now, this is what smart people do. But the kid hasn't moved. It's like he's transfixed. Shit, I've got to get a handle on this. Each time I try to rein in my magic, it rebels. I try putting the blanket on it like last time, but I can't concentrate to hold the blanket in place because of the irritation of the water.

The ground shakes under my feet so hard I feel like I'm on an old rickety rollercoaster. Not even two feet away from me, the ground begins cracking under the boy's feet. He's frozen to the spot.

I want to tell him to go, but I can't get the words to form in my mouth. Before I can rush to push him out of the way, the ground begins to crumble and breaks out wide.

"What the..." The boy finally begins to move and pivots toward the others, but the ground cracks faster than he can run. It opens up beneath him and swallows him whole. His screams ring in my ears even after he's gone.

My God. I killed someone on my own team. How many others am I going to hurt before I die? The flame inside me flashes like the bulb of an old-fashioned camera. It's so bright and warm. That's when something clicks. Ria knows we're here. Shit, she's using the Water Artifact against me to make me implode.

Dammit, I'm tired of being everyone's toy. She won't get what she's looking for any longer. Forcing myself to concentrate, I grab the blanket once more and cover my disjointed and chaotic power. I embrace the pain that's attacking me and use it to fuel me instead of fighting against it like I've always done.

Taking the blanket, I wrap it around the three elemental threads and the natural reaper and healing power that's always been inside me. Tugging it down, I make sure it's firmly captured and nothing is leaking out. The power fights against it, and it's hard to clamp down, but I manage.

"Hey, are you okay?" Dax's voice startles me.

Damn, I hadn't even realized my eyes were closed. The power isn't coursing as hard, and it takes a second for me to realize I'm no longer shaking. "Uh... yeah." Shit, I killed another innocent person. "But I..."

"Don't." He touches my arm and squeezes ever so lightly. "You told him to move. We all knew what was going on. That wasn't your fault."

"No, it's the smart lady who rules this place." Damien's smile stretches almost his entire face, and he winks. "If I didn't want the Water Artifact so damn bad, I'd get to know her a little better."

Gross. Of course someone causing havoc would attract him. He's a freaking demon. "Just stop." But Dax and Damien are right. This wasn't entirely my fault, and blaming myself allows Ria to have control over me. "We need to get moving. She knows we are here."

"How do you know this?" Luke jerks his head back and narrows his eyes.

"Did you feel all of the magic in the air?" Damien turns to face him and swivels his hand. "Someone used the Water Artifact to attack her and throw her off balance."

"If she knows we're here, we need to get moving." Brad steps up, and his eyes are red as if he'd been crying. "We can't let Josh's life be lost in vain. She expects this to throw us off kilter and maybe even force us to retreat. We have to show her our strength."

The longer we wait, the more likely I'll have another episode and endanger someone else. "This ends tonight."

"Yes, but we need to stay close and coordinate our efforts." Dax stands in between Luke and me. The muscle in his jaw ticks.

The three boys and Brad nod, and Damien grins.

This is all fun and games for him. One day soon, I'm going to wipe that smug look off of his face, but that'll be after I get the Water Artifact. I need all hands on deck right now. "Let's get moving."

We all take off at a slow jogging pace. Dax leads us toward the fortress, and Damien hangs in the very back. I'm not sure why that makes me uneasy, but there is one thing I've learned; never trust a demon.

When we hit the last block of houses before the fortress, Melody and six other people are waiting for us.

Shit, has she decided to turn against me after all? I stop in my tracks, not sure how to proceed. However, I refuse to hide behind anyone, so I step in front of Dax and meet her head on. "What's going on?"

"Well, I told you I had your back." Melody glances behind her and nods. "I've found more people who are willing to fight alongside you."

"Are you serious?" I appreciate her efforts, but I don't want to cause any problems for them. They live here after all. "I can't ask that of you all."

An older man steps next to Melody and raises his chin. "You aren't. We volunteered and would be honored to fight amongst you."

"But why?" I'm threatening to take their livelihoods from them. I don't understand how they are okay with all this.

"Does it matter why?" Luke frowns, and his sounds tone disapproving. "We shouldn't turn down any fighters."

"It does to me." Times like these are the very ones I realize that Luke isn't the best leader. He only thinks of his people or his own agenda, not all of the realms or species. "These people live here and will have to deal with all the repercussions. I don't want to ask something of them that will make their life harder when this is all said and done."

"Don't be a fool." Damien cackles as he catches up to us. "This is why you're weak."

"No, it's why we want to fight with her." A lady I had seen several times in the market steps up front and glares at the two men. "We've been ruled by people who dictate to us what to do without concern for our wellbeing. The whole market is a ruse. Most of the money we receive from sales go to them. It's hard to make ends meet." The lady points her worn finger at me. "She's different. I've seen her kind spirit and willingness to help. This is the type of leader we need. Someone who cares for everyone."

"Oh, please." Damien pretends to gag and rolls his eyes.

"Well, I for one am not going to turn down help either." Brad scans the new arrivals and rubs his fingers over his lips. "Do you guys by chance know any other way Chris can sneak inside?"

"Yes, in fact we do." The older man rubs his hand along

the loose skin right under his chin. "I've served Ria for many years. There is a secret entryway that only the people who work for her know about. Luckily, I'm one of them."

"And how do we get there?" Luke arches an eyebrow and rubs his fingertips together.

"It's a tunnel that leads from the living room and takes her to this house right here at the end. It's vacant, and there is a reason for it. It's a way to escape or smuggle things in without anyone seeing since all eyes are on the fortress."

"Okay, Luke, Damien, Brad, and the crew go attack the fortress similar to last time. That's what she'll be expecting." Dax pulls out a knife and glances around. "That will give the rest of us the opportunity to sneak in undetected."

"Don't you think I should go with her?" Damien's eyes flash red, and his shadows creep out, one brushing my skin.

Damn, why are those things so freaking cold? "No, you can cause a lot of damage with your powers. You are one of the best ones to keep Ria distracted." Maybe if I stroke his ego, he'll relent faster.

"Hmmm..." He runs his fingers through his hair and chuckles. "Well played and true. That's fine. Let's get going."

Brad throws his arms around me and pulls me into a hug. "Be safe."

Wow, maybe he does still care about me a little.

The six of them walk off, leaving me with the Water people and Dax. "All right, let's go. There's no time like the present."

"Fine, but we can't go into the fortress until we know the other ones are in place and causing the distraction." Dax bites his bottom lip and sighs.

"We can hear it from the tunnel. It isn't deep, and you can hear what's going on above." The old man cringes. "That's one way she finds out stuff."

Why am I not surprised she eavesdrops? We just need to go. "Show us the way."

The old man pulls out the key and walks to the door at the back of the house. He has it open within moments and walks in, not turning on any of the lights.

I grab Melody's arm and lower my voice. "Are you sure all these people can be trusted?"

"Yes, I would never put you in danger." She reaches out and pulls me into her side. "None of the citizens here are happy, and these are the ones who've had enough and are willing to make a stand."

"Okay, let's do this." I walk through the door, following the man with Dax and Melody right behind me and the remaining six following after them. We follow the old man into the pantry that is off the kitchen, and he presses a button that's hidden at the bottom of the last shelf. A door creaks open, causing dust to fly over everyone, and cool, stale air from the tunnel hits my nose.

Great this is going to be fun.

"Don't worry. It's not a long tunnel." The old man enters the tunnel, and we are immersed in darkness.

I'm so glad that my eyesight is great, or I would be hurting. The others stumble behind me, and Dax grumbles. "Don't run into me. You're going to knock me over."

"Everyone calm down." Hell, I don't want to use my powers, but right now, I don't have a choice. Otherwise, someone is going to get hurt on the way over. I loosen the hold on the blanket and pull at the vibrant purple strand. Soon, my hand lights up, illuminating the tunnel.

"Oh, thank God." The old man sags with relief. "I thought we were going to have to find our way in the dark." He begins moving again, and I hold my hand high so everyone's path is lit. It's not long before shouts echo in the tunnel.

Something above us crashes, and the walls around us begin to vibrate.

"Get moving and quick. They've started fighting, so we need to get in." Dax's voice is loud, and he places his hand on the small of my back. "Let's get this done."

"Here we are." The old man stops when he comes to the door, and his hands shake as he puts his key into the lock.

"Walter, are you okay?" Melody places her hand on top of his.

"Yes." He sucks in a deep breath and opens the door.

Holy shit, we're in.

23

We step into a dark hallway, and there is no one to be seen. Our distraction must be working, and everyone is focused on our guys outside.

"Where do we go now?" The old man looks at me, his eyes full of worry.

I'm about to answer 'how the hell would I know,' when something comes over me. It's a pull that can't be ignored. I don't know what it is, but I'm at its mercy. I follow it and find that it's leading me toward stairs. There is a ghost of light there and something damp; almost as if the water is thicker here than the rest of the island.

"Where are you going?" Dax follows close behind me, holding two knives in his hands now.

"I'm not sure." The steps are made of a brown tile, and the railings are metal. Intricate circles weave in and out of the railing giving it an elegant feel. This fortress reminds me of the mansion back on Earth. I take each step slow, making sure that I'm as quiet as possible.

"Dammit, Chris." Dax glances behind us and huffs out a sigh. "We've lost everyone."

That might be a good thing. That way, they can all deny helping us if caught even though they'd have to explain why they're here. But those answers would be easier to come up with when I'm nowhere in sight.

When we reach the top of the stairs, the tugging becomes more of a jerk, leading me down the hallway on the side that has three doors. The room at the end of the hall stands wide open. There is a soft turquoise glow shining out of the room.

Holy shit, it's the artifact. My heart skips a beat. There is where she's kept it all along. The light begins to pulse just like a strobe light, and my feet begin moving faster.

"Stop. This could be a trap." Dax's tone is harsh and full of frustration.

If I could, I would, but there is no turning back now. "I can't." It's so hard to even get those two words out let alone anything else.

He turns to watch my back. "I'll be glad when this whole thing is over. Protecting you is a full-time job."

Even being preoccupied with the artifact, I find his lame attempt at humor irks me. When I get to the doorway, I discover the three bubbles of water hovering in the air, being held in a glass container. It's similar to how the Angel's Breath was held, but for some reason, this artifact radiates the most power. It slams into me so hard I almost lose my balance.

"Something strange is going on." Ria's voice is so loud I can clearly hear her upstairs. "The water isn't responding to me like it normally does. Go check the house, and leave no stone unturned."

Oh no. I better get the damn artifact before she gets up here. As I approach it, something slams into me, and my brain goes hazy and off balance.

"Come on, we need to hide." Dax scans the area, but her footsteps are already echoing up the stairs.

"Huh?" What is he talking about? Why would we need to hide, and for that matter, where are we? "How did we get here?"

Dax stills then turns to face me. "Are you playing some kind of joke?"

Why would I be joking? "Uh... no." I glance around the room and take in the crystal cylinder hanging in the middle of the room and the decadent crown molding that sets this room apart from anything else I've ever seen.

"Is it possible?" Dax grabs my arm and pulls me close to him.

"What the..." Then everything crashes back in. I had the artifact within grabbing distance, and I didn't take it. What the hell's wrong with me? "I couldn't remember why we were here or even about the artifact."

"She must have traps spelled around the artifact so no one can get to it." Dax shakes his head and then scans the room. "We've got to hide before it's too late."

"Well, well." Ria enters the room. Her hair is pulled back into a ponytail which makes her lavender eyes stand out more. Blood stains cover her clothing, and she stands in the doorway. "Look what we have here."

"I thought you were better than this." When I first met her, she seemed sane. Now she's unhinged.

"Oh, I tried the nice way, but that didn't work." She glances at the artifact and then back at me. "And now you've been able to cause havoc because of the present I gave you. I should have let you combust."

Talking her down won't be possible. She's ready for blood. The amulet warms on my chest and my magic begins moving. Adrenaline courses through me, but I won't be the first one moving.

"That was you being nice?" Dax moves so he's in between us. "You killed someone in cold blood."

Charlie pops to the forefront of my mind even though he didn't say the name. He's right, there is no redemption for her. She manipulates just like most everyone I've had in my life. "You didn't have to do that. I was going to leave." My voice almost cracks at the end, but somehow, I keep it together.

"Oh, please. Like he would have let you give up on the artifact knowing you'd die without it." Ria lifts her hand so fast it almost blurs, and suddenly the air in the room becomes thick with moisture.

"What the hell is happening?" Dax begins sweating, and wipes the back of his hand against his forehead.

"She's using her connection." What is she trying to do? The air is thick but doesn't bother me like it does him. "You're going to make all of us uncomfortable."

"No, just him." She squeezes her fingers together forming a tight fist, and he falls to the ground. "The elements don't affect us as much since we both are connected to it." She almost spits as she says the few words.

Hell, I'd rather not be connected to it and have a normal life. This isn't something I chose. "I wish that it wasn't the case."

"That's why you don't deserve it." She pulls out her sword and steps toward me. "Why you were chosen is beyond me, but it doesn't matter. You'll never get the last artifact. It all ends now."

This girl is freaking psycho. My power surges and the Water Artifact flashes in sync with them. I'm being tugged toward it once again, but if I want to survive, I'm going to have to contend with Ria for a minute.

Dax is laying down on the ground, almost comatose. It reminds me of the time in Hell when I was off kilter. His face is bright red like a tomato and appears to be overheated. I don't know how she's doing that with the water, but he's not going to be much help to me now.

She lifts her arm up and swings the sword hard at my shoulder.

I call out to the wind, and it blows so hard her blade hits the ground right beside me.

"You got lucky." Ria spins and kicks her leg out, nailing me right in the belly.

Dammit that hurts. I stumble back into the wall. Not wanting to give her time to react, I push off, and my hands immerse in flames. I rush at her and grab for her dominant arm, hoping to eliminate some of the sword attacks. But when I get close, she grabs my hands dousing them with water.

Her connection to the water irks me. She shouldn't have been able to do that.

"Not as easy as you thought, huh?" She chuckles then punches me in the side.

Using her momentum, I spin and elbow her in the head, causing her to crash on the ground.

After flipping on her back, she jumps, landing on her feet, and swings her fist toward my face.

Ducking, I ram her in the stomach, slamming her against the wall. Her head makes a loud thud as it bounces off it. Desperate for this to end. I head-butt her and watch her fall to the ground. She groans and lays face down right next to Dax.

My head is throbbing. Maybe that wasn't the smartest

thing to do. Now that my power is all pulsing and out of whack, the water element feels so strong that it's undeniable. I need it now to complete me and need to get it before Ria regains all her senses.

The problem is I don't know how to get around the memory spell. I take small steps, getting closer and none of the confusion hits. Soon, I'm right next to the display, and I lift the glass lid off of the podium. The three round drops of water that hover in the air twinkle, and as soon as I reach out to touch them, the water soaks into my skin and absorbs inside me, traveling straight to my core with the other elements.

Just like the others, the power rushes through me, my limbs filling with cool liquid and helping to contain the raging inferno inside me that seems to always be near exploding.

As the four elemental powers inside me merge, the ground quivers underneath me. The water from the ocean crashes loudly and rushes toward me. The wind blows and whips against the building, and the stars appear to be on fire. Even though I'm not outside, I can feel what each element is doing to celebrate finally being in sync with one another.

There are no noises from outside. The fighting has halted, and as I walk to the window, the waves are now at the fortress, ankle deep and receding, but the fighters are not fighting and are, instead, watching the show.

Dax moans at my feet and pulls himself against the wall. "You did it."

Even he can feel the difference in the air, and now I can see everything. The hair on my neck stands as I feel Ria rising as quietly as possible. She grabs the sword off the ground and moves so slowly there aren't any sounds to alert.

As she raises her arm to swing the blade, I turn and stare her square in the eye. Without moving, I set the floor underneath her on fire.

She squeals, and then she reaches out to the water to put it out.

The only reason I know is because she connects with me, and before I can squash it, the water appears to extinguish the flames.

Crap, how is she still able to connect to it? It's freaking inside me.

A huge smirk fills her face. "Huh. Lookie there."

None of this makes sense. I've got to figure out a freaking way to get out of here and still protect everyone. "It's over, Ria."

"Oh, no it's not." She raises her hand, and the power inside me surges.

No, this isn't supposed to happen now that I have all of the artifacts. It's because of her damn connection to the water. Since the turquoise magic is surging, the other elements respond by increasing in strength as well.

"What's wrong?" Ria cackles and tilts her head at me. "Is something causing you problems?" She runs at me and swings her sword at my feet.

At the last second I jump over the blade and kick at her chest. I hit her square in the center, and she stumbles back.

"You need to end this." Dax is standing against the wall, but his face is still red from whatever Ria did to him. "The longer you draw it out, the worse it'll be."

He doesn't have to tell me that twice. "I'm trying."

"She's not strong enough to take me." Ria laughs as she tugs at me once again and then rears back and swings her fist at my face.

Throwing my right arm up, I block her and shake the

ground underneath her. I can't cause too much commotion, or she'll fall through the floor and could hurt someone below.

"You think that will hurt me?" She laughs and charges at me.

Using the wind to propel her even faster at me, I spin out of the way which causes her to run head first into the wall. She bounces off and falls to her knees.

My reaper magic begins coursing inside me, and even though I'm not touching her, it reaches out and latches onto her. The suctioning begins, and she yells.

How the hell is this happening? I've always had to touch them in order for this to happen.

She thrashes on the floor, and tears stream down her face. "No, please no."

I'm not sure how to stop it, and I'm powerless. Soon, a coolness floats into me as her soul begins to leave her body. It's strange because it used to be icy cold, and now, after absorbing all the artifacts, it's a refreshing sensation. Now, it's clear that this is what was meant to be. I was unbalanced before, and both my reaper and healing powers were too much at one time. Now, I'm balanced and able to perform this the way any reaper can.

As the life fades from her eyes, I can't help but feel as if this is karma in the working. She killed my love, and now she must die.

Her body spasms one last time, and she passes through into her afterlife.

24

Her soul leaves me, but I can't believe what the last several hours have brought. Reaping Ria and absorbing the last artifact has finally brought the missing piece of the puzzle to light. Bringing people back to life after death brings an unbalance to the world just like Damien has done by preventing souls from crossing over into their afterlife.

Since I have the power of the artifacts and my own reaper and healing magic, I'm able to accomplish this now, but it should never be used unless in dire situations. Having these artifacts inside me requires me to think like the angel had taught me not so long ago. I have to put the lives of many in front of my own personal needs. I can cause the world to be unbalanced as easily as anyone else.

"Hey... Are you okay?" Dax touches my shoulder and turns me in his direction. "She deserved that ending."

"I'm not upset over her." Now I just want to finish this. I can't leave this realm knowing their livelihood has been taken with me. I'm pretty sure I know a way to fix this before I go. "We need to let everyone know the fight is over before anyone else gets hurt." It hurts to look at Dax now that I can see his crack so easily. It's getting bigger and bigger by the day, and I wish there was a way to fix it.

"You're right. Let's get going." Dax heads out the door, walking slower than normal, but at least his coloring is coming back.

We head down the stairway, and I move toward the main doors to step out in the light.

As I step outside, the two suns are rising. Both sides have their weapons down, and they glance my way.

"Thank God you're okay." Luke comes over and pulls me into a hug. "I've been worried about you. When the elements went crazy, I wasn't sure whether you won or lost."

I'm still not sure either at this point. "If you're asking if I got the last artifact, then yes, I did."

Tide steps out from the crowd, his fists clenched. "Where is Ria?"

"She met the fate she deserved." Dax's voice is loud and echoes against the walls.

"How could you say that?" Tide's jaw ticks, and he body quivers. "She was protecting our world. How are we supposed to live?"

For once, I have an answer for that. "I'm not going to leave you empty handed."

"Really?" Melody's tone is full of hope as she watches me.

"Yes, I'm going to charge your water." I head to the part of the island we had entered so many weeks ago. That's where they get the water they use for the market. That's where I need to focus most of the magic. "I'm heading there now. You'll still be able to live as you always have, but with someone in charge that will care for your well-being."

"What the hell does that mean?" Tide points his finger at me and sneers.

"It means that they are done with having to mend their clothes and pay over half their earnings to you in the form of taxes." What the hell is wrong with people? This is not okay. "If you can't promise that this will stop so they can afford to eat and have clothes, then I won't help you."

If looks could kill, I'd be dead. "And what do you get out of it?" He huffs, and the words are formed around gritted teeth.

"Nothing, but I want Melody to oversee the processes, and I'll be back to check in from time to time." She's the one person I trust here, and she has a good heart.

Melody grins, and she places her hand on her heart. "I'd be honored and will respect your wishes."

"All right. Then that's what we'll do. I'm going to go charge the water now before I head back home." I need to get back and deal with things I've put off for too long.

"Come on guys, it's time to head back," Brad calls out to everyone, and they join Dax and me along with Luke and Damien.

Not wanting to have any additional conversations right here in front of the Water people, I get ready to get back to Earth.

It doesn't take long before I'm at the pier we had come in on. I bend down and place my hands in the clear, cool water. The water power shimmers to life, and the power pours into my hands and into the water. It already knows what I want to accomplish, and within seconds, the water is charged for the next ten years.

When I stand, Dax already has everyone circled around him except Damien. Dax holds out his hand and grins. "Let's see how bumpy this goes with everyone."

———— • • • ————

After we appear on the mansion's lawn and Brad and his fighters leave, I turn to walk into the building, but a black shadow forms behind one of the trees.

Luke holds open the door for me, but I hold up a finger. "I'll be right there. I've got to take care of something first." I bet that's Damien coming to cash in on our deal. Little does he know that he'll be leaving empty handed.

A flicker of understanding flashes in Luke's eyes. "All right. I'd tell you not to do anything stupid, but I think you know what you're doing. Dax and I will wait for you in my office."

I'm ready to get this part over with. He needs to give me Beth and never bother me again. Making my way to the tree, I watch as the shadows form Damien right before my eyes.

He leans against the tree and winks at me. "So... now it's time for you to relinquish the artifacts to me." He removes the amulet from around his neck and holds it out to me. "I'm sure you want this."

Does he think that he can still bargain with me? He must be crazier than I realized. "No, I'm not paying you anything, but you're still going to give her to me."

"Like hell I will." He wraps his fingers around the amulet and snarls. "I guess your friend will never find true peace."

His cocky ass is going down. "Oh, yes she will. If you don't hand her over to me now, you won't be able to leave here alive." I'm tired of all of the bullshit.

He scoffs at me but takes a step back. "You don't have it in you." Lightning crashes right next to me, and he jumps back. "What the hell?"

"Give me her soul, and leave now, or you won't be

around for another day." His days of having the upper hand are gone. I now can control all of the elements.

Black smoke begins to billow around him. Dammit, he's trying to leave. I force the air around me to be still which prevents him from transporting.

"You..." His mouth drops open, and he glances around.

"Don't be stupid." He's not used to not having the upper hand. "If you give me the amulet and leave, never bothering me or Becca again, then I won't stand in your way. Otherwise, be prepared to cease to exist."

"Fine." He holds out the amulet to me and drops it in my hand. "This will be the last time you see me."

"I'm serious. If I see you any time after this moment, I will kill you." I don't want to have to deal with his manipulation any longer. He's done having a hold on me.

"Even though it's at my expense, you've changed a lot in the last two months." Fire flashes in his eyes once more, and he steps back, the shadows taking over his human form once more. "I won't cause any more problems, at least until the artifacts are free again." Then, he's gone from my sight.

After all this time, I finally have Beth's soul right here in my hands. Her frightened face stuck in this stone creeps into my mind. I need to let her out and fast. She deserves to have a normal afterlife; one filled with peace.

I call to the fire inside me, and my hand blazes, melting the stone holding her soul. When it drips down onto the ground, my black reaper magic spurs to life and begins sucking from my hand. A coolness once again fills me, and I can feel when Beth transitions to her ever after.

It's a bittersweet moment for me. One, my best friend is really gone now, but she's found peace. This has reaffirmed that the council has been lying to everyone. Reapers have souls, but they don't want us to know so we don't have any qualms taking life or passing judgement. We die just like humans, and our actions determine our afterlife. Right now, I need to rejoice that Beth has found peace and won't live in terror day after day any longer.

Now I need to help Becca so she can have the same fate. I close my eyes and locate Becca. She's standing in front of her family house once more, watching them like an outsider. I clear all of the obstacles between us and transport to her location.

This time, she must have felt as I appeared behind her because she turns her head, and tears run down her cheeks. "I don't know what's wrong with me."

Even though I didn't know whether I'd get the irrational or calm Becca, I wasn't expecting this. Yeah, I didn't mean to cause this, but it's still my fault. "It's because you aren't meant to be here. Your soul is fracturing."

Her shoulders sag, and she runs her hand through her limp, greasy blonde hair, taking a clump of it between her fingers. "So... there isn't anything truly wrong with me. I'm not losing my mind?"

"No, it's because your time here is done. Once you move on from here, you'll be back to normal." It's strange because as I speak the words, I know they're true. "These are the repercussions of overstaying on Earth."

"Then, I'm ready to go. I'm tired of feeling lonely and out of control." Her hazel eyes beg me for understanding, and she clasps her hands together in front of her. "Please, help me."

A shiver runs through me. This is Dax's future as well. I've got to fix it all. They all deserve better than this. "Of course. Are you ready?"

She nods and holds her hand out to me. "Please, I'm going out of my mind."

Once again, my power thrums inside, and I step next to her. I lower her to the ground so she's laying and won't fall.

"Thank you." She sprawls out on the grass and closes her eyes.

I place my hands on her chest, and it takes mere seconds for her soul to pass through me. Finally, she's found peace. I stand and transport back to Luke's office.

Dax is putting all of the weapons back in the hidden closet, and Luke is working on papers at his desk.

"Sorry it took longer than I expected." I avoid Charlie's body in the corner because first, I need to deal with the two of them before I make the big decision about Charlie.

"It's about damn time." Dax scowls at me as the light shines through his soul even brighter.

"What's gotten into you?" Luke arches an eyebrow and points at him. "You're acting different."

"His soul is fracturing like Becca's." I'm so tired that I don't have time to sugar coat all of this. "Since he died, his being here is causing an unbalance. He will spiral away just like Becca did."

"So how do we fix it?" Dax's tone is full of angst. "I don't want to go down that same road."

"Someone needs to reap you again so you can finally land in your resting place." The words feel like sandpaper as they pass through my throat, but he deserves to know what's going on. Becca thought she was going crazy. I don't want him to have to endure that.

"But I still need him." Luke throws his pen on the table and stands. "We still have a lot of work to do."

"It's easy to be selfish when you aren't the one being impacted." What is it with all of these people? I'm the youngest one in this room, but it sure doesn't seem that way considering how everyone is acting. I need to help Dax. "I can reap you if you're ready."

Silence descends upon us, but Dax shakes his head no. "I'm not ready. Not yet. I still have some time, and I need to help Luke clean up the council. When I get bad, I'll ask you to do it then."

"That's true. Luke is going to need help." I hate to admit it, but Dax isn't nearly as bad off as Becca, so he does have more time.

"Yes, I need help getting the corrupted elders off the council." Luke places his hand on the table and bites his lip. "Are you going to resume your abilities now that you're back? I could really use your help."

"The temptation would be too strong to the other elders and Brad's council if I didn't step down." I've had enough drama, and the less I have to deal with people manipulating me for their own personal gains, the better. "No agency or person should have direct access to this power inside me. For some reason, I was destined for this, but I can't let it corrupt me."

"But think of all you can do..." Luke lifts both hands up and shivers.

"See what I mean. You need to find someone else to take over my spot." Even being this close to me gets him excited about what I can do. "Clean up the current council, or I will do it for you."

He swallows hard, his Adam's apple bobbing. "I'll get on it." He glances at Charlie and then back at me. "Dax, there is no time like the present. Do you want to go tell the other elders what happened?"

"Yeah, let's do it. After all that's happened, I could use some entertainment." Dax hugs me and heads out the door.

When I'm all alone, my eyes go to Charlie. My time is

running out, but I don't want him to go through what Becca did. I make my way next to him and touch his hand. It's cold as ice which is just wrong. He's warm and comforting, not stiff and frozen. I don't know how to go on without him.

The artifacts' strands, reaper magic, and healing powers begin coursing through me at the same time. All of the other times this happened were when they were rebelling because I was unbalanced. But now, with the addition of the water, they are moving in harmony.

A light flashes inside me, and then I realize what I have to do. If I'm willing to entangle my soul with his, it'll prevent the fracture from occurring. This can only be done once because if it's done too many times, my soul won't be strong enough to hold the power inside me. I push it out toward him, allowing the healing power to take a small chunk of my soul. We'll be linked forever, but I'm okay with this; he's my one and only.

When my power floods into him, it courses throughout him and brings his soul back. As soon as it comes back, I see that it's already cracked, but my healing power mends his soul with my piece. It covers his crack and latches on to his, blending them into one. As soon as it's pieced together, my powers return to me.

He's silent for a moment, but then his chest begins to move, and his hazel eyes open. He blinks a few times and then glances around. "Chris?" His voice is weak.

"Yes?" I take his hand and squeeze it. I hope he's going to be okay with me bringing him back.

"Am I alive?" He sits up and looks around. "Wait... Are we back on Earth? But the Water Artifact."

"It's over. I found the artifact, and now I'm whole." My palms become sweaty. Maybe I made a mistake. "You died, and I found a way to bring you back whole."

His face turns thoughtful, and then he throws his arms around me. "Thank God. I've been wanting to get back to you the entire time." He pulls me against him and kisses my lips.

"Also, I found Beth and released her soul." He needs to know this. She's his sister after all. "She finally has peace."

"I love you so damn much." He brushes the hair back from my face and grins. "Thank you. Knowing she has a chance for happiness brings me comfort."

Speaking of comfort... "Are you ready to go home? I'm tired of adventures and want to sleep in my own bed."

"I'll do anything with you as long as I get to stay by your side." He stands and takes my hand. "I'm ready when you are."

For the first time in my life, I can do whatever I want to do. I'm finally in charge of my own destiny.

The End

ABOUT THE AUTHOR

Jen L. Grey is a *USA Today* Bestselling Author who writes Paranormal Romance, Urban Fantasy, and Fantasy genres.

Jen lives in Tennessee with her husband, two daughters, and miniature Australian Shepherd. Before she began writing, she was an avid reader and enjoyed being involved in the indie community. Her love for books eventually led her to writing. For more information, please visit her website and sign up for her newsletter.

Check out my future projects at my website. www. jenlgrey.com

ALSO BY JEN L. GREY

The Marked Dragon Prince Trilogy

Ruthless Mate

Marked Dragon

Hidden Fate

Shadow City: Silver Wolf Trilogy

Broken Mate

Rising Darkness

Silver Moon

Shadow City: Royal Vampire Trilogy

Cursed Mate

Shadow Bitten

Demon Blood

Shadow City: Demon Wolf Trilogy

Ruined Mate

Shattered Curse

Fated Souls

Shadow City: Dark Angel Trilogy

Fallen Mate

Demon Marked

Dark Prince

Fatal Secrets

Bloodshed Academy Trilogy

Year One

Year Two

Year Three

The Half-Breed Prison Duology (Same World As Bloodshed Academy)

Hunted

Cursed

The Artifact Reaper Series

Reaper: The Beginning

Reaper of Earth

Reaper of Wings

Reaper of Flames

Reaper of Water

Stones of Amaria (Shared World)

Kingdom of Storms

Kingdom of Shadows

Kingdom of Ruins

Kingdom of Fire

The Pearson Prophecy

Dawning Ascent

Enlightened Ascent

Reigning Ascent

Stand Alones

Death's Angel

Rising Alpha

Printed in Great Britain
by Amazon